EL DORADO

THE ROAD TO EL DORADO

JUNIOR NOVELIZATION

adapted from the screenplay by

Peter Lerangis

DREAMWORKS

GOLD AND GLORY

THE ROAD TO
EL DORADO

PUFFIN BOOKS
Published by the Penguin Group
Penguin Putnam Books for Young Readers, 345 Hudson Street,
New York, NY 10014, U.S.A.
Penguin Books Ltd, 27 Wrights Lane, W8 5TZ, England
Penguin Books Australia Ltd, Ringwood, Victoria, Australia
Penguin Books Canada Ltd, 10 Alcorn Avenue, Toronto, Ontario, Canada M4V 3B2

Penguin Books Ltd, Registered Offices: Harmondsworth, Middlesex, England

Published by Puffin Books,
a division of Penguin Putnam Books for Young Readers, 2000

1 3 5 7 9 10 8 6 4 2

TM & © 2000 DreamWorks
All rights reserved

ISBN 0-14-130712-9

Printed in the United States of America

Prologue

El Dorado.

It is a place long remembered but never seen. The ancients called it The City of Gold—built by gods, not humans. It arose from the earth itself, perfect and pure. Its golden temples shone like the sun; its waterways flowed clear and bottomless.

According to legend, those who lived there were three-times blessed: With tremendous wealth, for gold was as plentiful as water. With happiness, for they lived during the Age of the Eagle, under the rule of kind and generous Chief Tannabok. And with peace, for their city was hidden from invaders, deep in the South American jungle. Above all, the greatest of El Dorado's riches was love and friendship.

Many have searched for the ancient city, but not a sign has been found.

Some say El Dorado was destroyed by a high priest of dark magic, the dreaded Tzekel-Kan. Others claim it remains in the jungle still. Hidden. Waiting.

Perhaps the truth will never be known. But the legend remains...

one

CHIEF TANNABOK WAS SMILING.

Smiling.

The High Priest, Tzekel-Kan, hated that smile. So content. So peaceful.

So ignorant.

Peace, he knew, was not to be trusted. Peace made people happy. Happiness made them lazy. Laziness made them weak. And the weak were always crushed—just as Chief Tannabok and his adoring citizens would be crushed.

Tzekel-Kan had read the mystical signs. They were written clearly in his codex, a sacred book of magic. The Age of the Jaguar was at hand, a time of glorious evil. Soon the gods themselves would be visiting El Dorado, including a powerful conquering Dark God. Without a strong leader, the city of gold was doomed.

Tzekel-Kan had called the citizens to the ancient ceynote well, the gateway to the spirit world. There, at the seat of all magic in El Dorado, he would offer the gods two sacrifices and give Chief Tannabok one last chance to back down.

His voice boomed out over the well: "For a thousand years, the gods have blessed this city with peace and happiness. But now that time is coming to an end. The gods will come and cleanse this city—with blood! And sacrifice."

From the crowd, Tzekel-Kan brought forth two captives. One was a local townsman who had not sufficiently kowtowed to Tzekel-Kan. The other was a raven-haired young woman named Chel.

Chief Tannabok faced the priest fearlessly. He had heard Tzekel-Kan's warning before. "Enough," he replied. "We do not know that the gods will demand sacrifice."

As if in answer, the moon slowly began to edge across the sun. A frightened hush swept through the gathered multitude as El Dorado was plunged into darkness.

Tzekel-Kan glared triumphantly at Chief Tannabok. "The omens are clear—behold! Do not doubt the prophecies."

"I don't," Chief Tannabok replied. "I doubt *you*. If the gods have a problem with the way I've ruled this city, let them appear and speak for themselves!"

"And so they shall!" As Tzekel-Kan drew his knife from its sheath, Chief Tannabok flinched.

But the High Priest turned away from him, toward the

well. With a quick, sharp slice, Tzekel-Kan cut his own hand with the knife. Drops of blood fell steadily into the well. But this was no ordinary blood. From its flow, a mystical orb appeared, floating above his outstretched palm.

"I SUMMON THE GODS TO EL DORADO!" Tzekel-Kan proclaimed.

Chief Tannabok shivered. He could feel the magic grow. It made the air hum and the water in the well begin to swirl. Soon the spell would be borne into the heavens and the underworld.

The gods, he knew, would hear.

As legend has it, the magic reached across the world too. To the shores of Spain.

There, a cruel, conquering warrior was about to set sail. His ships were clad with thick armor and heavy weaponry. His destination was a place known only by legend. A place he planned to call his own.

The city of El Dorado.

two

"TODAY WE SAIL TO CONQUER THE NEW WORLD—FOR SPAIN! For glory! For gold!"

The voice of Hernan Cortes boomed out across the seaside village. It echoed off the whitewashed houses, drowning out the powerful hoofbeats of his warhorse, Altivo. His band of warriors followed on horseback, shooting rifles toward the blazing Spanish sun.

Townspeople in the midst of afternoon chores stopped to watch. Cries of "VIVA CORTES!" greeted the warriors as they thundered toward the waterfront.

With conquest and glory on their minds, none bothered to look at the Wanted sign posted on a nearby wall. None paid attention to the faces that glowered from the sign—two men known as Tulio and Miguel, wanted for cheating money from wealthy Spanish citizens.

No one knew that the two men were right under their

noses—crouched in a game of dice by the dock.

As always, Tulio and Miguel were winning. And as always, their game had drawn a large crowd. The village men gasped at their uncanny skill, while the young women tried to catch their glance.

The dark, dashing Tulio was the craftier of the two. Beneath his humor and charm was the personality of a rascal. He adored gold. Its smell was perfume to him, its jingling the sweetest of all music. He preferred to win his money from the wealthy and corrupt—and his trusty loaded dice had never failed him.

Only one thing meant more to Tulio than gold and jewels: his friendship with Miguel.

To Miguel, money wasn't the point. *Excitement* mattered—the wandering life, music and laughter, crowded towns and windswept beaches, the loving arms of beautiful señoritas, and the thrill of the chase whenever his and Tulio's schemes were discovered. Miguel's sunny smile and long golden locks cast a spell over people. Wherever he went, they welcomed him with open arms.

The two men were a perfect pair. Without Tulio's cunning, Miguel's life would be dull. Without Miguel's honest looks, Tulio would be in jail. Where one traveled, so went the other. Always. It was their pact. They were partners.

Today they were united against a sailor named Zaragoza, whose tremendous greed was matched only by the size of his appetite—and of his belly.

As Tulio held the loaded dice, carefully blowing on them for good luck, Miguel smiled. Soon the money would be all theirs. He and Tulio would skip town with full pockets, onward to new adventures.

"Seven!" Tulio cried.

Miguel leapt up and slapped him a high five. "All right, partner!"

"*Tons of gold for you—hey! Tons of gold for me—hey!*" they chanted together. "*Tons of gold for we—*"

"Hey—one more roll!" shouted Zaragoza.

"Uh, guys? You're broke," Tulio said. "You've got nothing to bet with."

Zaragoza grinned. Reaching into his jacket pocket, he pulled out a rolled-up sheet of paper. "I have this—a map of the wonders of the New World."

Tulio was unimpressed. "A map?"

"Let's have a look!" Overcome with curiosity, Miguel grabbed the map. In the center was a drawing of a magnificent city labeled El Dorado. "Tulio, look! El Dorado! The city of gold! This could be our destiny—our fate!"

"Miguel," Tulio said under his breath, "if I believed in fate, I wouldn't be playing with loaded dice."

Miguel's face fell. He cast a droopy, puppy-dog glance at Tulio.

Tulio fought the urge to give in. He hated when Miguel did this. Tulio was a sucker for his friend's sad expressions. "*Not with the face,*" he warned. "No. No. No, no, no, nope, no—"

Zaragoza snatched back the map. "I said one more roll! My map against your cash."

Miguel kept staring at Tulio, his expressions changing by the moment: pouting...eager...pleading...trusting... hopeful...

It was too much. Tulio couldn't say no. He turned back toward Zaragoza, whose gargantuan frame was puffed out menacingly. "All right, Pee Wee, you're on!"

"This time," Zaragoza said with a grin, "we use my dice."

Oops.

Glaring at Miguel, Tulio mouthed the words, "I am going to kill you."

"*Me?*" Miguel mouthed back.

As Tulio began to roll, Miguel picked up a guitar. With a sharp flick of the wrists, he strummed a dramatic flamenco tune.

Tulio gulped. He wasn't used to using *real* dice. He needed a pretty girl to blow on the dice for good luck, but there were no takers in the crowd. So Tulio blew on them himself.

Miguel strummed louder, making a huge racket.

"Stop that!" Tulio shouted.

Miguel froze. The circle fell silent as Tulio rolled the dice. All watched breathlessly as the cubes tumbled into the circle and landed on...

"Seven!" Tulio shouted with relief.

Miguel jumped. "Yyyyyes!"

"Well, nice doing business with you!" Tulio said to Zaragoza, stooping to gather the money and the map.

From his shirt pocket fell another pair of dice. They clattered to the ground—a perfect seven.

Zaragoza glared at Tulio. He pounded the ground hard. The dice jumped—and landed on seven again.

Zaragoza pounded and pounded. Each time the dice flew upward, tumbled around, and landed.

Seven...

Seven...

Seven...

Seven.

"I knew it!" Zaragoza growled. "Your dice are loaded!"

Tulio had a plan for situations like this. Tulio had a plan for everything. He shot a look of shock and betrayal to Miguel. "You gave me *loaded dice*?"

As the crowd advanced toward Miguel, Tulio backed away, preparing to bolt. But an angry guard stood in his path, blocking his retreat.

"Guard, arrest him!" Tulio blurted out, pointing to Miguel. "He gave me loaded dice!"

"You dare to impugn my honor?" Miguel shouted, pretending to be insulted. He turned to the constable indignantly. "*He* was the one who was cheating. Arrest *him*. He tricked those sailors and took their money!"

"Oh, now *I'm* the thief?" Tulio exclaimed. "Look in the mirror, pal!"

Miguel pulled the guard's sword from its sheath. "*En garde!*"

"*En garde* yourself! I will give you the honor of a quick and painless death!" Tulio swiped another guard's weapon. He thrust it upward dramatically.

Its blade glinted in the sun—barely. It was a puny, stubby dagger.

Tulio quickly tossed it aside. "But not with that!" Swiping a longer sword, he thrusted it angrily at Miguel. "I prefer to fight fairly. Any last words?"

"I will cut you to ribbons, fool!" Miguel retorted.

"Such mediocrity! Let your sword do the talking!"

"I will! It will be loquacious to a fault!" With a guttural cry, Miguel lunged toward his friend.

Tulio leaped aside and thrust again. "Ha! You mincing, prancing twit!"

The two men jumped onto the top of the wall that surrounded the plaza.

"Ha! You fight like my sister!" Miguel yelled.

"I've fought your sister—that's a compliment!"

Clank! Clank-clank!

As the crowd cheered them on, Miguel swept his sword upward, a savage, high blow. Tulio blocked it, just in front of his nose. "Not the face," he warned. "Not the face."

Miguel quickly thrust again. He flicked the sword from Tulio's hand, then caught it skillfully. He had both weapons now. He pressed his sword against the defenseless Tulio.

A hush swept over the plaza.

Suddenly both men turned to the crowd. "Ladies and gentlemen," Tulio announced, his voice suddenly calm, "we've decided it's a draw."

"Thank you all for coming," Miguel added. "You've been great. See you soon!"

The crowd was stunned. Without waiting for a response, Tulio and Miguel leaped over the wall. They fell to the other side in a gale of laughter.

"Congratulations," Miguel exclaimed.

"That was good," Tulio replied. "Very good—"

A sudden snort made him freeze.

They were in a large, dirt pen. And the bull who lived there did not seem happy to have company.

His eyes were bloodshot. His hooves were pawing the ground.

Miguel swallowed. "Uh, we should have kept those swords, I think."

"I've got a plan," Tulio whispered.

"What is it?"

"Well, you pet him…"

"Yeah?"

"And I'll…*run!*"

As they scrambled for the fence, the bull charged.

three

TULIO AND MIGUEL VAULTED OVER THE FENCE. The bull didn't bother. He crashed right through and raced after them, his hooves pounding the packed-dirt road.

"There they are!" a voice echoed. A guard raced out of the plaza, followed by a crowd of angry townspeople.

Tulio and Miguel darted through the town, ducking into a narrow alleyway.

Shhhlunk.

The bull jerked to a stop, wedged between the buildings.

At the other end of the alleyway the two men stopped short at a dead end. There was no turning back. The crowd was approaching fast.

A clothesline hung just above their heads. They grabbed it and swung upward, landing on a high balcony.

Peering over the rail, they saw a waterfront loading dock. Directly below them were two large, open barrels.

"I'll bet we can make that," Miguel said.

"Two pesetas says we can't," Tulio replied.

Silently they jumped, plummeting downward, wind-milling their arms. Each landed in a barrel with a dull thud.

"You lose," Miguel said through a hole in the side.

With a sigh of resignation, Tulio pulled two pesetas out of his pocket and tossed them into the other barrel. They yanked the lids closed and huddled in cramped silence, the sounds of the mob now far above them.

Soon the angry voices faded away. But before Tulio and Miguel could decide what to do next, the barrels began to move upward, as if lifted by a rope.

"Miguel, what's happening?" Tulio called out. "Miguel?"

"We're both in barrels," Miguel said. "That's the extent of my knowledge."

The barrels swung widely in the air, then came down. They landed on a wooden floor with a hollow thud.

"Okay, Miguel," Tulio called out. "On three, we jump out and head for the dock."

"Good," Miguel replied. "Okay. Excellent."

Together they counted, "One…two…"

Whomp.

Something heavy landed on top of the barrels.

"Three!"

They pushed, but the lids didn't move.

"Three!" they shouted again, pushing harder, grunting with the effort—but they couldn't budge them.

"Three...!"

"Three...!"

"Three...!"

They refused to give up. Whatever was up there must have been huge.

But that wasn't their only problem. They were rocking, swaying. They could hear the distant screech of seagulls, the flapping of sails. They were on a ship—heading for who-knew-where.

Frantically they kept trying to push the lids off, until finally they collapsed in frustration. The barrels were hot and stuffy, and all they could hear were their own loud, exhausted breaths.

As the sun began to set, Miguel summoned his last bit of strength. "You ready?" he called out.

"Okay, one more," Tulio replied.

"One..." they chanted together, "two...three!"

Once again they rammed their shoulders up against the wooden boards—and this time, they kept going. The lids popped off. Bursting out of the barrels, Miguel and Tulio gulped in fresh air. They were free!

Sort of.

They were in the cargo hold of a ship. Along with Hernan Cortes's crew. They had just removed a heavy chest from the top of the barrels—and they were not amused by what they'd discovered underneath.

Miguel and Tulio were now officially stowaways.

"Excuse us," Miguel squeaked, shrinking back down into the barrel. "We're out of here…"

Tulio quickly improvised an excuse. "Okay," he said brightly, "who ordered the, uh…pickles?"

The sailors rushed forward. They yanked Tulio and Miguel out and clapped them in chains and wooden stocks.

Moments later, the two men were dragged straight to the cabin of the ruthless conqueror.

Cortes was enormous. His shoulders were like an ox's yoke, his legs like sturdy barrels. He wore a suit of armor, which seemed almost dainty on his massive frame.

Glowering at Miguel and Tulio through slitted, sinister eyes, he said, "My crew was carefully chosen, and I will not tolerate stowaways. You will be flogged. And when we put into Cuba to resupply, you will be flogged some more and then enslaved on the sugar plantation for the rest of your miserable lives." He turned to his guards. "To the brig!"

Flogged. Enslaved. The words made Tulio seize up with fear.

But not Miguel. "All riiiiight!" he called out gleefully. "Cuba!"

Bonk. Bonk. Bonk. Bonk. Bonk. Bonk. Bonk. Bonk.

Tulio banged his head against the wall of the brig. The banging helped him think. He needed an escape plan, and fast.

Tulio hated the stuffy little room under the main

deck. It smelled of fish, and its only opening was a ceiling grate in the deck above.

Miguel was no help. He was asleep.

Bonk. Bonk. Bonk.

From above deck, a rough voice said, "Hey, Altivo!"

Tulio peeked up through the grate. A sailor, holding a basket of apples, was walking past Cortes's warhorse.

As the horse tried to grab an apple, the sailor pulled away. "Not for you! You're on half-rations, orders from Cortes!"

An apple fell from the basket, and Altivo lunged after it. But it rolled away, falling through the grate and onto Miguel's lap.

Miguel snapped awake. "So!" he blurted out, casting an anxious glance to Tulio. "Um, how's the escape plan coming?"

"All right, all right, wait! I'm getting something!" Tulio gave the wall one last *bonk.* "Okay, here is the plan. In the dead of the night, you and I grab some provisions, hijack one of those longboats, and then we row back to Spain like there's no mañana."

"Back to Spain?" Miguel asked. "In a rowboat? *That's* your plan, is it?"

"That's pretty much it," Tulio replied confidently.

"Great. Sensational. I like it. So, how do we get on deck?"

Tulio's face went blank. Under his breath, he began reviewing his plan: "In the dead of night…you and I grab some provisions…hijack one of those longboats—"

Miguel groaned. Tulio hadn't thought through the hardest part! "Oh, great…"

"Well, okay, what's *your* idea, smart guy?" Tulio snapped.

"Don't ask me. *You're* the one with the plans!" Miguel grabbed the apple, prepared to take a bite, and stopped. "Wait. I have an idea. Come on, give me a boost."

Tulio cupped his hands under Miguel's foot, lifting his friend upward. Miguel pressed his face to the grate. "Here, Altivo!" he called out, holding the apple through the bars.

The horse cocked his head.

"You want a nice apple?" Miguel said sweetly. "Come and get it!"

As Altivo walked over, his eyes hungrily aglow in the moonlight, Miguel withdrew the apple and put it in his pocket. "But you have to do a trick for me first," he said.

Altivo whinnied with frustration.

"All you have to do is find a pry bar," Miguel continued. "A long piece of iron with a hooky thing at the end?"

"Miguel!" Tulio shouted, struggling to keep his friend aloft. "You're talking to a *horse*! He can't understand *pry bar*. There's no way—"

Through the grate came a flash of metal. Something landed on the floor with a clank—a set of keys.

Miguel grinned triumphantly.

"Well," Tulio grumbled peevishly, "it's not a pry bar."

He set Miguel back down on the floor. Together the two friends unlocked the cell.

By now, night had settled and all the crew members had retired to their cabins. Quietly Tulio and Miguel raced up to the deck and collected food and drink. Then they dashed toward the nearest lifeboat, which hung suspended on a winch.

The horse followed their every move. As they stopped by the railing, he nuzzled Miguel.

"Oh, Altivo," Miguel said with a fond smile, "thank you. Listen, if we can ever return the favor—"

"For Pete's sake, Miguel, he's a ruthless warhorse, not a *poodle*," Tulio hissed. "Come on, before he licks you to death!"

The two men hopped into the boat, tucking the container of food into the bow. As they began to lower the boat to the water, Altivo gazed over the railing and whinnied loudly.

"What's the matter with him?" Tulio asked.

"He wants his apple," Miguel replied.

"Well, give it to him before he wakes up the whole ship!"

Miguel took the apple from his pocket and tossed it upward.

It flew over the railing and bounced off the ship's sail. Shooting past a sleeping night watchman, it caromed off the mast and the telescope—then hurtled right back down, over the ship and into the waters below.

Without thinking, Altivo dived after it.

Miguel's eyes widened in horror. "Altivo!" he cried out, leaping after the horse.

"*MIGUEL!*" Tulio let go of the rope. The boat dropped to the water with a bone-jarring splash.

Tulio immediately took the oars and began rowing toward his friend. "Miguel, have you lost your mind?" he shouted.

But Miguel was swimming toward Altivo. "Hang on, old boy! Help is coming—"

A shadow loomed over his head—another ship in Cortes's fleet. Sailing right toward them.

Miguel and Altivo frantically swam away. Tulio pulled his oars against the billowing sea. He felt the boat rise upward on a wave…and upward…

It teetered at the top, then plunged downward, spinning in the air. Screaming, Tulio fell into the ocean.

He emerged under the boat with Miguel and Altivo, caught in a pocket of air between the water and the upended floor of the boat. "Loop the rope under the horse!" Tulio yelled.

He and Miguel grabbed ends of the rope, tied it around Altivo, and swam back upward.

They broke the surface on a swelling, choppy sea. "On the count of three, pull back on the rope!" Tulio commanded.

"What?" Miguel shouted.

The ship was upon them now—massive, cutting swiftly through the sea, sending up a sudden, violent wake.

"Three—*pull*!"

The wave rocked the lifeboat hard. Tulio and Miguel fell back in the water, still clutching the rope.

And the boat flipped.

So did Altivo. He was still in the boat, on his back, his legs sticking straight up in the air.

"Hey, it worked!" Miguel shouted.

He and Tulio swam to the boat. They hoisted themselves in and sprawled out, exhausted.

"Did any of the supplies make it?" Tulio asked, breathing hard.

"Well…" Miguel looked accusingly at Altivo. "Yes and no."

Altivo sat up. His cheeks bulged. For a horse, he looked terribly guilty.

Tulio was furious. If Miguel had just given the horse the apple, Altivo wouldn't be here, and none of this would have happened. Now they had no compass, no direction, no clue—and nothing to eat. And a horse to look after. "Oooooh, great," he murmured.

"Tulio, look on the positive side!" Miguel shouted. "At least things can't get—"

KAAA-BOOOOM!

With a crack of thunder and a flash of lightning, rain began pouring down into the boat.

"Excuse me," Tulio said, "were you going to say, '*Worse*'?"

There went that rosy notion. "No…" Miguel murmured.

"You're sure?"

"Absolutely...not. I've revised that whole thing."

"We're at least in a *rowboat*," Tulio suggested.

"We're in a rowboat," Miguel agreed. "Exactly!"

The storm raged through the night and the entire next day, tossing the boat about as if it were a toy. Miguel and Tulio took turns at the oars as a frightened Altivo shivered in the aft.

Weeks passed, the stormy weather giving way to hot days and still nights. The boat drifted aimlessly on a sea that never seemed to vary. Land was nowhere to be seen. Without water, Tulio and Miguel's lips became parched, their voices hoarse and scratchy. Without food, they were gradually weakening.

What was worse, the boat was crowded and uncomfortable. Tulio could not stretch out to sleep. Finally one sweltering day he'd had enough. "Ahhh, ditch the horse!" he demanded.

"Ohhhh, I like the horse," Miguel replied.

"Ahhh, he's too heavy."

"Ohhh, he's cute."

At that moment a seagull alighted on their oar, tired and ready to drop.

Delirious with hunger, Tulio poised to grab it. He felt himself salivate. Right now, the scrawny little bird looked like the answer to a dream.

But before he could lunge, a shark burst out of the ocean and snagged the bird in its jaws.

Tulio fell back into the boat, his last drop of hope

gone. In his mind, this had to be a sign—they weren't going to make it.

Throwing his head back to the blazing sun, he cried out the first words that came to mind: "I want my mommy!"

As the sun rose on the next morning, its light was dulled to a soft gray by the mist. Tulio and Miguel sat back to back, on the edge of wakefulness but too tired to move. Their hands drooped lifelessly over the side of the boat. Altivo lay still, his chin resting on the starboard ledge.

Miguel's face was sunburned, his eyes nearly swollen shut. In a barely audible voice, he rasped, "Tulio, did you ever imagine it would...end like this?"

"The horse is a surprise," Tulio replied, still bitter about Altivo.

Miguel closed his eyes, not expecting to open them again. The sun's light burned through his eyelids, depriving him of the comfort of darkness. "Any...regrets?" he whispered.

"Besides dying?" Tulio thought hard. "Yeah...I never had enough gold."

"My regret—besides dying..." Miguel swallowed, trying to relieve his sandpapery throat, "...is that our greatest adventure is over before it began, and no one will even remember us."

Tulio's voice grew soft and sincere. "Well, if it's any consolation, Miguel, you made my life an adventure."

"And if it's any consolation, Tulio, you made my life rich."

Altivo rolled his eyes.

He didn't understand humans. They argued, they fought, they stirred up trouble—but they never told each other how they *really* felt.

Until a time like this.

four

PAIN.

Blinding whiteness.

Tulio had to squint as his eyes flickered open. Was *this* what death felt like? Hot and bright, silent and still?

He was too exhausted to lift his hands out of the water.

But his hands weren't in the water. His fingers were brushing against something solid, not liquid. Something gritty and dry. Something like…

Sand.

Tulio sat up. Miguel was awakening too. They looked at their hands blankly, not quite believing what they saw.

"Is it?" Miguel asked.

"It is!" Tulio shouted.

They gazed upward in amazement. A beach stretched out before them, sloping gently upward to a dense jungle.

"*Laaaaaand!*" The word burst from their mouths together. With sudden strength, they leaped out of the boat and fell to the beach.

"Mwah!" Tulio cried, kissing the sand with glee.

"Mwah!" Miguel joined him. Together they crawled up the beach, their heads bobbing giddily as they kissed and kissed....

"Mwah!" "Mwah!"

"Mwah!" "Mwah!"

"Mwah!" "Mwah!"

Suddenly Miguel stopped. He'd planted his lips on something smooth and hard.

He looked up—and came face to face with a grinning, whitewashed skull.

"AAAAAAAGHHHH!"

Tulio and Miguel sprang to their feet, stunned. There were *two* skulls—attached to two skeletons, embedded with war clubs.

"All in favor of getting back in the boat, say aye!" Tulio cried out. "*AYE!*"

"AYE!" echoed Miguel.

"*AAAYYYYY!*" whinnied Altivo.

All three ran back toward the boat. Tulio began pushing it into the water.

But Miguel stopped short. A soft, strange whistle sounded behind him. He looked over his shoulder. The noise was coming from a large, oddly shaped rock.

It reminded him of something—something on

Zaragoza's map. Quickly Miguel drew the map out of his pocket.

From the shore, Tulio called out, "Miguel, I could use a little help! Hello?"

Altivo, eager to go, grabbed an oar in his teeth and offered it to Tulio.

But Miguel's attention was fixed on a strange symbol on the map. It was shaped exactly like the whistling rock—and it marked the beginning of a long, hand-drawn path, near an area that corresponded to their cove.

"Tulio, we've done it!" Miguel waved the map. "It's all right here!"

Tulio let go of the boat. "You still have the *map*?"

"The whistling rock…" Miguel gazed around, searching for the next symbol: "The stream—"

"You kept the *map*, but you couldn't grab a little more *food*?"

"…Even those mountains! You said so yourself—it *could* be possible. And it is! This really is the map to El Dorado!"

Tulio stared at Miguel as if he'd lost his mind. "You drank seawater, didn't you?"

"Come on!" Miguel urged.

"I'm not *coming on*!" Tulio replied, turning away. "I wouldn't set foot in that jungle for a million pesetas!"

Miguel thought fast. He knew exactly how to reach Tulio—through the very thing Tulio loved most. "What about a hundred million?"

Tulio spun around. *"Whaaat?"*

"I just thought that, after all, since El Dorado *is* the city of gold…"

"What's your point?"

"You know—dust, nuggets, bricks? A temple of gold where you can pluck gold from the very walls?" With an exaggerated sigh, Miguel began rolling up the map again. "But *you* don't want to go. So let's get back into the boat and row back to Spain. After all, it worked so *well* the last time—"

"Wait. Wait a minute." Tulio fell into deep thought—and Miguel knew he had him hooked.

"New plan!" Tulio blurted out. "We find the city of gold. We take the gold. Then we go back to Spain."

"And *buy* Spain!" Miguel exclaimed.

"Yeah!" Tulio shouted.

"That's the spirit! Come on, Tulio, we'll follow that trail!"

Altivo cocked his head and gave Miguel a look.

"What trail?" Tulio asked.

"The trail that we blaze!" Miguel reached down to one of the skeletons and grabbed its sword. Brandishing it fiercely, he swiped at the underbrush.

A branch fell away, revealing a rock wall.

Miguel pointed in another direction. *"That* trail that we blaze!"

As he charged off into the jungle, Altivo shook his head apprehensively and backed away.

Tulio gave him a warning glance. "Oh, no, you

don't…" Grabbing the warhorse by the bridle, he followed after Miguel.

But Altivo was not going to give in easily.

"Yeow!" Tulio cried out. "Miguel, your horse bit me on the butt!"

With the map as their guide, they plunged into the jungle. The trees grew thick, the vines dense. Shadows skittered underfoot. Sudden screeches pierced the eerie quiet.

Altivo chafed at his bit—and Tulio didn't blame him.

But Miguel kept them going. After the awful boat journey, he felt alive again. Here, finally, was adventure. Mystery. Danger. His face buried in the map, he followed the twisted path, looking for the next symbol—a flying hawk.

At a sudden, skittery sound in the underbrush, he froze. An armadillo raced across their path, chased by a snake. Miguel flipped the snake aside with a thrust of his sword.

From that moment on, the two men had a new partner. The grateful armadillo stayed by their side, scampering along after butterflies. They named it Bibo.

Perhaps Bibo was a good omen. As they stepped under a huge rock overhang, a shaft of light penetrated through a hole in the rock. A hole in the shape of a flying hawk!

Miguel whooped with joy. They were on the right track for sure.

One by one, the signs appeared to them, just where the map said they'd be:

A weeping woman…

A rock that looked like a woman's face, above a cascading waterfall.

A fire-breathing dragon…

A rock promontory, shaped like a dragon, out of whose mouth burst a flock of birds.

The path led through cool grottoes and dense trees, along meandering streams and into clearings dappled with sunlight. Fearlessly Miguel forged ahead, sticking to his path. He followed it around a large, deep-blue lagoon, barely looking at the water.

Tulio couldn't resist. He dived right in, inviting his friend to join him.

Before long they were all splashing in the water—even Altivo and Bibo.

Thwwick! Thwwick! Thwwick!

Suddenly Tulio felt stinging sensations, head to toe. He screamed in pain, flailing his way to the shore. As he rose out of the water, Miguel gasped.

Dangling from Tulio's body were dozens of brown, slimy leeches.

As Miguel pulled off the bloodsuckers, one by one, Tulio groaned about the unfairness of it all. Miguel nodded sympathetically, but he had to hold back a smile. Tulio may have carried loaded dice, but sometimes he had the bad luck.

Soon they hit the trail again, looking for the next

symbol, a large, sharp-toothed fish. But when Altivo trotted off on his own, the two men raced off the path after him—and found him in a natural hot tub, surrounded by bubbling warm water.

Surely leeches wouldn't survive in that heat—but humans could. Tulio and Miguel stripped off their clothes and jumped in.

Closing their eyes with joy, feeling relaxed and rejuvenated, the two men did not see a band of monkeys swing through the trees and land near their piled-up clothing.

As the monkeys tore off screeching into the jungle, shirts and pants in hand, Tulio and Miguel snapped back to reality.

"Hey!" Naked and dripping, they took chase.

Altivo and Bibo sat back and enjoyed the sight. Humans worried about the silliest things.

After retrieving their clothes, Tulio and Miguel forged onward, looking for the sharp-toothed fish. Approaching a stream, they walked around carefully, examining the deep water.

Splooosh!

Tulio didn't see the monstrous, scaly creature leap out of the water—but he felt its jaws clamp on his behind.

As he screamed bloody murder, Miguel leaped into action, grabbing the fish by the tail and pulling it off. With a shout of triumph, he held the fish aloft—one more symbol had been found!

Tulio did not share the joy. He hobbled along, rubbing his sore spot. Grimacing, he tried to look on the bright side—the deeper into the jungle, the closer to El Dorado.

Tulio and Miguel walked for days, pulling Altivo after them, checking off each symbol as they came upon it. With Tulio by his side, Miguel could concentrate on the map. With Miguel by his side, Tulio could regain courage after his accidents. Whatever happened, they knew they had each other—partners to the end. And that made the going easier.

Before long, the dangers didn't scare them anymore. They sang and told stories, keeping each other's spirits up. They laughed at Bibo's antics. At night, they slept under the stars.

Finally only one symbol remained: El Dorado itself. On a bright, crisp day, they searched for the city, warbling at the top of their lungs. They felt giddy with anticipation as they climbed a narrow hill.

Suddenly the ground rumbled beneath them. They looked down and saw the jungle floor, far below.

They were on an overhang, not a hill.

And they were way too heavy.

With a sickening *crrrrrack*, the earth split. They scrambled back, but it was too late.

The ground fell out beneath them.

They fell, flailing, crashing through the foliage until they landed hard in a heap at the bottom.

five

TULIO AWOKE.

He was sprawled on the soft jungle floor. Awake. Alive and unhurt. Miguel, Altivo, and Bibo were beside him, still unconscious.

The map had landed on his face. He yanked it off.

He scanned the area around him: a cliff, rising up through the shadow behind them...a small clearing...a roaring waterfall....

Looming above it all, near the waterfall, was a giant stone monument. Its surface was decorated with strange figures, carved into the smooth stone. Tulio squinted his eyes at one of the symbols—two men, perhaps ancient gods of some sort, riding on a horse.

"Hmmmm..." Tulio grabbed the map and ran his fingers along the trail. Where it ended, deep in the woods, were a waterfall and a monument. Next to the monument were the words *El Dorado*.

This was it. Their goal.

A block of carved stone.

Tulio's heart sank. For *this* he had nearly lost his life?

Miguel was the one who'd led them here. Miguel was to blame. Tulio tried to contain his mounting anger as he glanced at his partner, unconscious on the soft earth.

"Miguel?" he sang out. "Miguel, wake u-up! We're the-e-ere!"

His eyes springing open, Miguel jumped to his feet. "We've found it?"

"Ohhhh, yeah," Tulio said, seething. "We've found it."

"*Fantastic!* Where is it? How far?"

"Right here."

"Where? Behind the rock?"

"No, no. This is it."

"Give me that!" Miguel snatched the map from Tulio. He walked around the rock, looking desperately for a further clue. "But—the—I—this can't—"

"Apparently 'El Dorado' is native for '*great...big... ROCK!*'" Tulio said, practically spitting out his words. Swinging around, he mounted Altivo. "Hey, I'll tell you what—I'm feeling generous, so you can have my share."

"You don't think Cortes could have gotten here before us and—?"

"And *what*?" Tulio snapped. "Taken all the really *big* rocks? The jerk."

"Tulio, we have to think about this. I mean, we've come all this way and we should really—"

"Get on the horse."

"You're right," Miguel conceded with a heavy sigh. He glanced at Tulio, pouting and droopy-eyed.

"No, no, no. Not with the face!" Tulio shouted. "Stop!"

Reluctantly Miguel climbed on behind Tulio, who was now staring at the map, trying to find a way out. "It looks like there's a path right over there…"

Neither of them saw the figure emerge from the waterfall.

She was a young woman. Her hair, long and black, flashed in the sunlight as she ran. Her outfit, two swatches of white and pink material, showed her shapely curves. Tucked under her arm was a head carved out of solid gold.

Tulio and Miguel both felt their blood rush. After days in the lush jungle, they had seen unimaginable beauty. But none of it approached the magnificence of this gorgeous stranger.

She had not yet seen them. As she ran, she looked anxiously over her shoulder….

Thud.

Bumping into Altivo, she fell backward. The golden head went flying.

Tulio and Miguel jumped.

FOOOOOOOSH!

With a thunderous noise, an army of native tribesmen exploded through the cascade as if springing to life from the water itself.

They were angry and armed with spears. And they were chasing the girl.

Tulio and Miguel froze. The girl scrambled to her feet, scooping up her statue.

But the soldiers stopped short. Their mouths dropped open, their eyes widened—as if they'd seen something fierce and awesome.

Although their spears were pointed at the young woman, their faces were raised to the monument—at the carved etching of the two gods, mounted on a horse.

Thinking fast, the young woman tossed the golden head up to Tulio. She turned back to her pursuers, empty-handed.

Tulio trembled as he held the carved head. It was the most exquisite thing he'd ever seen—solid gold, worth more money than he could imagine. Was this what the men were after? "Hello?" he squeaked.

Distracted from the monument, the warriors suddenly pointed their spears at him.

Tulio flung the golden head back at the native girl—but she tossed it right back.

Tulio attempted a smile. "Is—is this your rock?"

No answer. Just scowls. And pointy, flesh-ripping spears.

Tulio took that for a yes. He and the young woman passed the head back and forth, like a game of hot potato, the warriors following its path with their weapons.

Finally Tulio missed. The statue bonked him on the head and fell to the ground. "Sorry!" he blurted out, sweat pouring down his forehead. "W-we were just look-ing. We're tourists. *Tour...ist?* We—we lost our group. May we go now? Heh...spears!"

The young woman finally snatched up the golden head, and the soldiers grabbed her. They signaled Tulio and Miguel to follow them back toward the waterfall.

Altivo walked lightly, fearfully. Tulio and Miguel exchanged a glance of sheer panic. Trying to escape now would be foolish. All they could do was obey.

The men guided them onto a dirt path that circled behind the falls. There, a river ran under an archway of piled stones, ancient and crumbling—and beyond it was a dark tunnel. At the mouth of the tunnel lay a long, flat boat.

The warriors gestured with their spears toward Tulio and Miguel, urging them into the boat.

Shaking, the two men climbed in. The young woman followed, then Altivo and Bibo.

Pushing against the river floor with long poles, the tribesmen launched the boat through the archway, into the darkness. All Tulio and Miguel could hear were the swish of water and the occasional grunt of a warrior. Faint outlines flashed by them on the walls—carvings? Drawings?

Tulio looked toward Miguel and saw only the whites of his frightened eyes. They were prisoners now. They could only wonder at their fate.

Try as they might, neither man could stop thinking about the two skeletons at the beach.

Soon a ray of light shone ahead. It was faint at first, but when they rounded the bend it hit them full force, blasting through a gated archway with such brilliance that they had to shield their eyes.

This was not the harsh white light of the noon sun. It was golden, with a warmth and brilliance like nothing Tulio and Miguel had ever seen.

The boat passed through the archway and into a large pool, surrounded by a marble walkway. As their eyes adjusted to the intensity, Tulio and Miguel gazed around in astonishment.

Faced with the realization of their dream, they could barely speak: "It's…it's…*El Dorado*!"

six

IN THEIR WILDEST DREAMS OF EL DORADO, Tulio and Miguel had imagined a radiant city, decorated with jewels and gold.

They hadn't dreamt wildly enough.

The temples shone as if the sun itself had painted the walls with its flame. Graceful buildings abounded, bedecked with vines that cascaded like water. Public plazas and wide streets teemed with people, busy and contented. The marble-rimmed pool was a vivid mirror that reflected the skyline, doubling its glory. Only one aspect marred the perfection, a massive volcano that loomed in the distance. But no one looked concerned. El Dorado seemed far removed from danger—a hidden jewel, strong and brilliant, surrounded by a ring of paradise.

And yet, as the boat approached a dock, people fell

silent, their faces fearful and wary. Two men dressed in warlike garb—one resembling an eagle and the other a jaguar—turned and ran in different directions. As if to give warning.

Tulio and Miguel exchanged a look. This was not promising.

The warriors docked the boat and gestured for Tulio and Miguel to climb out and mount Altivo.

As they did, the crowd parted. A path was clear now, leading to a grand temple at the top of a long set of stairs. The native guards led the way, surrounding Altivo. The young woman walked alongside.

"Well, it was nice working with you, partner," Tulio whispered into Miguel's ear.

As they approached, a figure emerged from the temple above them. "Behold!" he bellowed. "As the prophecies foretold, the time of judgment is now!"

The man was dressed in a red and yellow robe with an amulet around his neck, and he carried a long scepter. His chest was broad and muscular, and a stripe of red paint crossed his taut, sinister face. He had the sleek, sinewy look of a jaguar. "Citizens!" he continued. "Did I not predict that the gods would come to us?"

A gasp went through the crowd.

Tulio and Miguel both looked over their shoulders to see which gods he was talking about. But everyone else's eyes were focused on one place.

Them.

Slowly the man descended the stairs. He was followed

by another man, who carried himself regally, with a kind and intelligent look in his eye. Around his ample waist was a blue tunic of the finest material, on his head a golden crown that was shaped like the head feathers of an eagle.

"My lords, I am Tzekel-Kan," the first man said as he reached Tulio and Miguel, "your devoted High Priest and Speaker for the Gods."

Tulio didn't know what to say. How did a *god* talk? He cleared his throat and offered: "Hey."

"I am Chief Tannabok," said the other man. "What names may we call you?"

"I," said Miguel, in his deepest, most godlike voice, "am Miguel."

"And I am Tulio," Tulio chimed in.

"And they call us...Miguel and Tulio," Miguel added dramatically.

Tzekel-Kan grinned widely. "Your arrival has been greatly anticipated."

"My lords, how long will you be staying in El Dorado?" asked chief Tannabok.

"I see you have captured this temple-robbing thief!" Tzekel-Kan said, cutting off the chief's question. "How would you have us punish her?"

The woman thought fast. Holding the golden head toward Tzekel-Kan, she pleaded, "My lord, I am not a thief! See, the gods sent me a vision to bring them tribute from the temple, to guide them here. My only wish is to serve the gods."

Tzekel-Kan gave Tulio and Miguel a questioning look.

Even in his frightened state, Tulio recognized the young woman's technique. She was smart. She was clever.

She was a lot like him.

"Release her!" The sound of his own command startled Tulio. He gave an uneasy glance to Tzekel-Kan, who wasn't moving. "Don't you think?" he added.

Tzekel-Kan let go of the woman, obediently but with reluctance. "You will begin by returning this to its rightful place," he commanded her.

The woman darted away, up the temple steps.

"Forgive me, my lords," Tzekel-Kan said.

Tulio and Miguel smiled at each other. They could get used to this.

"My lords," Chief Tannabok spoke up, "why do you choose to visit us?"

Tzekel-Kan scowled at him. "Enough! You do not question the gods!"

"That's right!" Miguel shouted, puffing out his chest grandly. "Don't question us—or...or..." He searched his mind for something fearsome, something to make them quake in their sandals. "...or we shall have to unleash our awesome and terrible power! And you don't want that!"

Tulio looked at him in horror. Leave it to Miguel to go way overboard.

"Well," Tzekel-Kan replied, "yes...we do!"

Miguel deflated. "You do?"

"Of course we do!" Tzekel-Kan said, gesturing toward

the chief. "Visit your wrath upon this nonbeliever! Show us the truth of your divinity!"

"Divinity?" Tulio squeaked. "One moment."

He pulled Miguel aside, out of Tzekel-Kan's earshot. He almost tripped over Bibo, who was chasing a butter-fly.

Grrrrrommmmmm...

The distant volcano suddenly rumbled, shaking the ground. Gasps of shock washed over the crowd.

Tulio barely noticed. He was focused on something more important—getting himself and Miguel out of this situation alive. "Miguel," he said through clenched teeth, "you know that little voice people have, that tells them to quit when they're ahead? *You don't have one!*"

"Sorry, I just got carried away." Miguel shrugged. "Maybe we should tell the truth and then beg for mercy. They might—"

"Are you nuts? We'd be butchered alive!"

"Well, what does *your* little voice say?"

"It says shut up and let me think!"

GRRRRROMMMMMM...

The volcano began spewing smoke and spitting embers.

"Yes, but they're getting suspicious," Miguel barreled on, "and if we don't come up with some sort of mega cosmic event, my friend, in the next five seconds I think we'll find ourselves—"

"I'm trying! I'm trying!" Tulio snapped, dodging Bibo again. "I can't think with all these distractions!"

Miguel knew the way Tulio's mind worked best—with a little healthy head-banging. He began slapping Tulio's forehead, hard. "Would you hurry? Faster, Tulio! Think think think—"

"Horse, horse!" Tulio blurted out.

Miguel rolled his eyes. That was the answer to the *last* emergency....

"I'm on the verge of—" Tulio felt Bibo crash into his ankle once again, interrupting his thoughts. This was the final straw.

"*WILL YOU STOP*?" he cried out to the armadillo.

His voice echoed throughout the plaza. "STOP... OP...OP..."

The volcano quieted.

An abrupt, eerie silence settled over El Dorado.

All eyes were on Tulio now. One by one, the natives dropped to their knees. They prostrated themselves in gratitude.

Tzekel-Kan led a raucous cheer. A band of soldiers joined him, all dressed in tunics that suggested the darkness and stealth of a jaguar.

Fear vanished from Tulio's and Miguel's faces. Breaking into smiles, they held up their arms in triumph. They strutted forward, giddy with relief, through the adoring crowd.

Tulio laughed aloud. He and Miguel were gods now—all because of a coincidence. They had ultimate power. And ultimate power was...well, fun. As they passed a sour-looking guard, Miguel made a snarly face. "Don't make me start it up again—because I *will*."

The guard fainted.

The chief looked stunned as Tulio and Miguel approached. He bowed his head humbly.

"O mighty lords," Tzekel-Kan intoned, "come let me show you to your temple!"

"All riiiight—*temple*!" Miguel shouted.

As Tzekel-Kan turned to go, he came face to face with Chief Tannabok. "Step aside," he muttered.

The chief stood his ground for a moment, then moved away.

Tzekel-Kan passed, leading Tulio and Miguel. The chief fell in behind them, as did the young woman.

At one end of El Dorado stood a temple more resplendent than the rest. Tzekel-Kan and the chief climbed the stairs and flung open a set of curtains.

Tulio almost drooled.

Gold. Rubies. Emeralds. Diamonds. The cavernous room seemed to explode with light reflecting from the precious stones. Its furniture was brocaded with the softest silk, sewn with gold thread. Its walls held hanging hand-woven tapestries, its floors were covered with rich carpets.

And in the midst of it all stood two luxuriant thrones.

Tulio and Miguel felt light-headed. They had never *imagined* a room like this.

"To commemorate your arrival," Tzekel-Kan said, "I propose a reverent ceremony at dawn."

Chief Tannabok was not to be outdone. "Then perhaps *I* could prepare a glorious feast for you tonight!"

"Which would you prefer?" Tzekel-Kan demanded.

Neither Tulio nor Miguel had a clue. They looked at each other.

"Both?" Miguel suggested cautiously.

"Both," Tulio agreed.

"Both," Miguel announced.

"Both is good," Tulio confirmed.

Tzekel-Kan and Chief Tannabok backed away, bowing. "My lords," they said gravely as they made their exit.

Outside the temple, Tzekel-Kan turned to the chief and grinned evilly. "And so dawns the Age of the Jaguar. Happy New Year."

Neither Tulio nor Miguel heard the comment. When the two leaders were gone, they burst out laughing.

"Tulio!" Miguel whooped. "Tulio, they actually think we're *gods*!"

"It's an entire city of suckers!" Tulio exclaimed, practically dancing with joy. "We just have to keep this up long enough to load up on the gold and then get out of here."

Altivo chuckled at the antics. But his face suddenly fell as he spotted a movement behind a potted plant.

It was a person—an intruder. He tried to signal to the two men.

But Miguel was in heaven. He jumped up on the throne, throwing his arms wide triumphantly. "We'll be living like kings—Miguel and Tulio!"

"Tulio and Miguel!" Tulio corrected, leaping up next to him and flexing his biceps.

Miguel threw his arm around his partner. "Mighty and powerful gods!" they both shouted as they practiced a few powerful-god poses.

Altivo let out a warning snort—and an unexpected voice broke their celebration:

"Hello?"

Tulio and Miguel whirled around toward the potted plant. From behind it stepped someone they did *not* want to see—the young woman. She had been listening to them the whole time.

And she knew their secret.

seven

TULIO THRUST OUT HIS CHEST, PROPPING HIS
LEG ON THE THRONE ARM. "Depart, mortal," he
intoned, "before we strike you with a lightning bolt."

The young woman rolled her eyes, humming nonchalantly.

"Beware the wrath of the gods—be gone!" Miguel
shouted, waving his fingers at her and making sounds
like lightning: "*Dzzzzt! Dzzzzt!*"

"Save it for the high priest, honey," the woman said.
"You're going to need it."

"*Dzzzzt! Dzzzzt!*" Miguel repeated, louder.

"Miguel," Tulio said, "it's not working. We've been
caught."

"*Dzzzzt! Dzzzzt! Dzzz—*"

"Oh, don't worry about me," the young woman said,
stepping away from the thrones. With a smirk, she said,

"My only wish is to serve the gods, remember?"

"How?" Tulio asked suspiciously.

"If you want to get the gold," she said, "and you don't want to get caught, you're going to need my help."

Miguel sneered. "What makes you think we need *your* help?"

The woman waved her fingers in a mockery of Miguel's lightning gestures. "'*Dzzzzt! Dzzzzt!*'" she imitated. "Are you serious?"

Altivo snickered.

"Okay," Miguel said, "so, who are you?"

"What's your angle?" Tulio asked.

"No angle," the woman replied. "I want in."

"In?" Tulio repeated.

"On the scam," the woman replied.

Tulio forced a laugh. "There's no scam. Why would you think there's a...Why?"

"So I can get out," the woman said.

Miguel leaned toward Tulio and muttered, "I thought she just said she wanted in."

"She wants in so she can get out," Tulio said.

"Ah, got it," Miguel replied. He turned to the woman with new confidence. "Why?"

The woman sighed. "You think you're the only ones who dream of better things, of adventure? You've got your reasons, I've got mine. Let's not make it personal, okay? It's just business."

Tulio and Miguel were impressed. "Oooh," they exclaimed.

"So when you guys are ready to go back to wherever you came from, I'm going with you."

Tulio's admiration vanished. It was one thing to like this girl—and a whole other thing to trust her. "No. Don't think so," he shot back.

"All right, fine," the young woman said with a shrug. "After all, I'm sure you know the proper rituals for blessing a tribute…the holiest days on the calendar…oh, and of course you know all about Xibalba. Okay, good luck! See you at the execution!"

Rituals…executions? At the sound of the words, Tulio and Miguel lost their regal bearing. As the young woman turned to leave, Tulio ran around to block her path. "Wait! Hold it!"

She met his glance levelly, then held out her right hand. "Deal?"

"Deal!" Miguel blurted out.

"Not yet." Tulio put the kibosh on their handshake. "Let's just see how this works out."

"Uh-huh." The woman opened up her left hand. "Well, then, I suppose that means you'll want these back."

In her palm rested Tulio's dice.

"How'd you get those?" Tulio exclaimed.

"And where was she keeping them?" Miguel asked, eyeing her skimpy outfit.

The woman smiled. "Call me Chel. Your new partner."

As she ran off to an inner room, Tulio called out, "That's partner in *training*!"

Chel emerged with an armful of royal garments. "Now put these on. Your public is waiting."

The material was smooth and silken, the colors deep and rich. It made Tulio and Miguel's own rough, sun-bleached cloth feel like sacks.

Tulio immediately began to change his clothes—until he saw that Chel was still in the room.

"Do you *mind*?" he exclaimed.

Chel's face turned red. "Oh. Excuse me. 'Bye!"

Miguel watched her leave...and kept watching as she went down the stairs...and as she walked across the plaza. "Maybe," he said rapturously, "they should call this place *Chel* Dorado...."

Uh-oh.

Tulio had seen this a hundred times already. Miguel was falling in love.

"Whoa, whoa!" Tulio said. "She's big trouble."

Miguel spun around. "What?"

"The little voice? Remember the little voice? For just a second—imagine that you have one. What would it be saying about Chel?"

Miguel thought a moment, then raised a mischievous eyebrow. "'Ooh-la-la'?"

"No!" Tulio said. "Listen—*WE* are partners. *WE* have a plan."

Miguel took a deep breath. Tulio was right. First and foremost, they stuck together. It was how they got into this, and it would be the only way to get out. "Get the gold. Go back to Spain."

"Yes! And we are *pretending* to be gods. Now … put Chel in the mix. What's the voice saying?" Tulio cupped his hand to his ear. "Listen carefully."

"Chel is off-limits?"

Tulio smiled with relief. At last Miguel got it—no girlfriends, no distractions. "Bravo! Chel is off-limits! Shake on it."

Miguel clasped his hand. Of course Tulio was right. Without the partnership, nothing worked.

"Besides, we're supposed to be *gods*," Miguel said with a knowing wink. "We must avoid giving in to temptation!"

Tulio smiled at his friend. Now it was time to face the people of El Dorado—as gods. Turning toward the temple entrance, he strode forward. His foot caught on the hem of his tunic, and it slid off his shoulder. "This is going to be tougher than I thought," he murmured.

"Relax," Miguel told him. "Just smile, act godly, and follow my lead!"

They stepped out the door. The entire city was gathered below. Chief Tannabok signaled a band of musicians to begin a song.

As Tulio and Miguel descended the stairs, the townspeople began to cheer. A mother thrust a baby up to Tulio for a blessing. Tulio made a funny face and tickled it—and the baby bit his finger.

Trying to hold back a grimace of pain, Tulio hurried down the steps after Miguel. The surrounding cheer grew to a roar as the two men mounted Altivo and rode through the streets.

Miguel and Tulio smiled and waved, soaking up the attention. Wherever they looked, groups were paying tribute. One set of people walked across hot coals, dressed as Miguel and Tulio. Others thrust gifts upward—trinkets and jewels and handicrafts.

At first the two friends felt funny about all the attention, all the gifts. But they quickly got over it. After all, the people *wanted* them to be gods—so why disappoint them?

Graciously they accepted the tributes. And the jewels.

And, of course, the drinks offered to them by Chief Tannabok, in the humongous goblets.

Early next morning, sunlight hit their faces like a slap. Tulio and Miguel groaned in agony. Memories of the party swirled in their heads—at least until the drinking part. It was all fuzzy after that.

Tzekel-Kan and Chief Tannabok had pulled back the entrance curtains. "Good morning, my lords!" Tzekel-Kan announced, leaning over Tulio and Miguel with an oily grin.

"He's back," Miguel muttered.

"Oh, no," Tulio grumbled.

The curtain closed again. Tulio and Miguel could hear Tzekel-Kan addressing the crowd: "The gods have awakened!"

A great cheer went up.

They were all there. All of El Dorado. Waiting.

Tulio and Miguel stumbled out of their beds. The god thing wasn't over yet. It was a new day.

Frantically pulling themselves together, they thrust aside the curtains and strode down the stairs. Their heads ached. As they waved to the adoring throng, every muscle hurt. Chel went before them, strewing flower petals in their paths.

"Psst, hey, Chel," Tulio hissed. "What's going on?"

"It's not going to be good," Chel replied, shaking her head.

She led them to the great ceynote well. There, Tzekel-Kan stood on a ceremonial ledge that jutted over the deep water.

"The city has been granted a great blessing! And what have we done to show our gratitude—a meager celebration? The gods deserve a proper tribute!"

Miguel and Tulio exchanged a nervous glance.

"The beginning of a new era," Tzekel-Kan continued, "demands *sacrifice*!"

The crowd parted. A group of guards came forward, pushing a figure wrapped in cloth toward Tzekel-Kan. When they reached the High Priest they began to unwrap the man.

Sacrifice?

Human?

Tulio and Miguel blanched. They hadn't expected anything like this.

Finally uncovered, the man knelt by the edge of the well. He was trembling.

"I don't like this," Tulio murmured.

"Tulio, we've got to do something!" Miguel said.

Tzekel-Kan strode toward the prisoner, lifted his sword high, and prepared to strike.

eight

THERE WAS NO TIME TO THINK. Tulio stepped forward. "STOP!"

His voice echoed across the well. Tzekel-Kan froze.

All eyes turned to Tulio. Quickly he drew himself up, deepening his voice and offering a strong rebuke: "This is not a proper tribute!"

"You do not want the tribute?" Tzekel-Kan asked, lowering his sword.

"No, no, no—we *want* tribute!" Miguel blurted out, trying to cover up Tulio's act of mercy. "It's just that..."

· His voice trailed off. Out of the corner of his eye, he saw the prisoner beginning to waver by the edge of the well. Miguel ran to his side—and the grateful, beleaguered man collapsed in his arms.

The crowd was waiting for Miguel to finish his sentence. He gave Tulio a desperate glance. "Tulio, tell him!"

"The stars are…" Tulio's mind dug deeply—and quick. "…Not in position for this tribute!"

"Like he says," Miguel piped up. "The stars…can't do it…not today."

"Perhaps it is possible I misread the heavens?" Tzekel-Kan asked, crestfallen.

"Don't worry about it," Miguel said, patting him on the back. "To err is human, to forgive is—",

Tulio slapped him on the head. Miguel was getting carried away again, ignoring the little voice.

"My lords," the chief interrupted, walking toward them with a warm smile, "may the people of El Dorado offer you *our* tribute?"

He turned away to reveal a throng of beautiful women, approaching Tulio and Miguel with armfuls of gold.

"My lords, does this please you?" the chief asked.

Girls? Gold? What else *was* there? "Yes, very nice," Miguel said, managing to keep his tongue from dangling out of his mouth. "Certainly acceptable."

"Lovely," Tulio quickly agreed. "It'll do."

"The gods have chosen!" Chief Tannabok beamed at Tulio and Miguel. "To Xibalba?"

"XIBALBA! XIBALBA! XIBALBA! XIBALBA!" the crowd chanted.

"No. No!" Chel shouted.

But neither Miguel nor Tulio heard her. Swept up in the moment, they shouted, *"To Xibalba!"*

"XIBALBA! XIBALBA! XIBALBA! XIBALBA!"

Chel cringed. "Ohhhh, great..."

The native women veered toward the well. Then, still chanting, they began tossing the gold into the water.

In shock, Tulio began following the tribute, like a lemming heading heedlessly to the edge of a cliff.

Miguel yanked him back, calling out to Chel, "Hey, what are they doing?"

"They're sending it to Xibalba," Chel explained, "the spirit world."

"*Spirit world*?" Tulio shouted.

Chel looked from one to the other, hoping they would take charge. But the two men were completely stupefied.

She knew *she* would have to save the gold. Quickly coming up with an idea, Chel raced over to Chief Tannabok. "Ahem. Excuse me, Chief. The gods have... changed their minds about Xibalba. They wish to...bask in the reverence that has been shown them."

The chief cocked his head with surprise, then turned to address the women: "*Stop!* They wish to bask! Take the tribute to the gods' temple!"

In obedience, the women turned back. Miguel breathed a sigh of relief.

Tulio was nearly weak with gratitude. He glanced at Chel, in awe and admiration. Any lingering doubts he'd had about her were gone.

"Nice going," he whispered.

Miles away, on the beach at the edge of the jungle, a fleet of ships sailed in. Had Miguel and Tulio seen the

Miguel and Tulio—partners and best friends—
wander the streets of Spain in search of adventure.

"I knew it! These dice are loaded!"

"*Let your sword do the talking.*"

"*I've got a plan. You pet him…and I'll run!*"

"In the dead of night, you and I hijack one of those longboats…"

"You want a nice apple?
You have to do a trick for me first."

"Tulio, did you ever imagine it would end like this?"

Following the map through the jungle

"It's...it's El Dorado!"

The chief and Tzekel-Kan vie for the new gods' favor.

The opposing team

Chel gives Miguel and Tulio a new ball—Bibo!

Tzekel-Kan conjures the stone jaguar to life.

The jaguar chases Miguel and Tulio through
the streets of El Dorado.

A dramatic escape through the gateway to El Dorado

fleet, they would have recognized it instantly.

They had escaped one of the ships not long ago.

They were Cortes's ships.

Cortes himself stepped out onto the shore. His eyes lit on the washed-up lifeboat and the footprints that led into the jungle.

"Well, well, well," he said, "what have we here…?"

"Tons of gold for you—*huh!* Tons of gold for me—*huh!* Tons of gold for we—*huh!*" chanted Tulio and Miguel gleefully, as they were carried back to the temple atop a luxurious litter. Around them, the townspeople danced and sang jubilantly.

It was all theirs now—officially, legally. All the gold they'd ever dreamed of.

"Not bad for a day's work, eh?" Tulio gloated.

"No. Not bad at all," Miguel replied.

"We just became richer than the king of Spain!"

"Speaking of kings, the chief and High Priest seem a bit…tense. You know, I'm not sure they get along."

Tulio chuckled. Good old Miguel had a clear grasp of the obvious. "Listen, all we have to do is keep playing one against the other—you know, do a little god-dance, chant some mystic mumbo jumbo, dazzle 'em with some smoke and mirrors, and then get the heck back to Spain."

Miguel gazed back at the heaps of gold. "Tulio, how are we going to get all this back to Spain?"

Tulio chuckled again at Miguel's naïveté.

But he had no answer.

He hadn't thought that far.

It took Tulio the rest of the morning to concoct a plan. It was a good one. Foolproof. But they would need a boat big enough to fit them and all their gold.

They paid the chief a visit in his temple and carefully detailed the new plan. He listened carefully, his quizzical expression growing into bafflement. "A *boat*?" he asked.

Tulio nodded. "Yeah."

Miguel cringed. In their haste, they hadn't realized a major flaw—all-powerful gods didn't *need* boats. "We really hate to be ascending so soon," he chimed in, "but some urgent business has come up—family matters, you know."

"Yeah," Tulio agreed. "Yeah, family."

Chief Tannabok nodded sadly. "We expected you to be staying with us for the next…thousand years."

"Well, as we say in the spirit world," Tulio improvised, "there's *your* plan and then there's *the gods'* plan. And our plan…calls for a boat."

The chief was looking at him as if he were crazy.

"We're going to ascend in kind of a horizontal pattern at first," Tulio added desperately, "and then we're going to go vertical as we get further out to sea."

With a heavy shrug, Chief Tannabok said, "To build a boat large and glorious enough would take about a week."

"A week?" Tulio echoed. They'd *never* be able to keep up the charade that long. There was only one way to make the chief move faster. Tulio would have to pit him against the High Priest. He leaned over to Miguel and murmured loudly, "I wonder how long it'd take Tzekel-Kan to do it?"

Chief Tannabok's face tightened. "But for the gods—three days!" he piped up.

"Well, if that's the best you can do," Miguel said condescendingly.

"Well..." The chief raised an appraising eyebrow. "Perhaps if you were not *burdened* with so much *tribute*, you could leave sooner."

Escape without gold? Tulio didn't like that idea. "I like it here, Miguel," he said quickly.

"Yep, yep, three days is just fine," Miguel agreed.

Back in the gods' temple, Tulio paced anxiously. The plan was flimsy. Maybe he and Miguel shouldn't wait for the boat. Maybe they should sneak out right away.

The chief had agreed to the plan—but he was no dummy. And neither was Tzekel-Kan. Sooner or later they'd catch on.

The question was, how soon?

"Three days is not fine—this is a real problem," Tulio said, idly tossing a pair of gold earrings up and down. As he paced past Chel, he handed them to her. "These go well with your...ears."

"Thank you," Chel said, flattered.

"Miguel, how are we going to keep this up for three days?" Tulio asked.

Miguel sighed. "You worry too much."

"No, I worry exactly the right amount," Tulio shot back, annoyed. "You can never worry too much. We just have to lie low—"

"But Tulio, this place is amazing!" With a dreamy expression, Miguel walked toward the floor-to-ceiling window that looked out over the city. "I mean, I wonder what's over—"

"No!" Tulio shouted. The window opened like a door—to Miguel, that was an invitation to wander. At this point, they needed to lay low, keep their mouths shut. One mistake could blow everything. "Don't even move!"

"Tulio," Miguel said, stepping toward the window, "you—"

"You're moving! Hey! Hey, hey! Uh-uh-uh! Just stand there."

Miguel froze, balancing on one leg. "For three days?"

"Yes. Exactly. For three days. Don't even breathe. All right?"

Miguel nodded.

"Promise?" Tulio asked.

"Yeah, yeah, yeah."

"Great. Good. Now, if you'll excuse me, I have to gloat over my gold."

With that, Tulio slipped into the next room. He hated to leave the gold alone for too long. It soothed him.

Chel stood by the window, gazing out. "It's beautiful, isn't it?"

Miguel sighed. "Are there really jeweled caverns here with walls of jade?"

"And so much more," Chel said with a crafty glint in her eye. "You know, you really shouldn't miss it."

"I couldn't," Miguel said, gesturing into the other room. "Tulio..."

Chel lowered her voice conspiratorially. "I'll cover you."

"Oh, good, thanks," Miguel said with a grin. Then, louder, he said, "Hmmm...so what happened to Altivo?"

"I don't know," Chel replied.

As she turned to look, Miguel darted out the window.

nine

TULIO WALKED INTO THE THRONE ROOM. His arms full of gold, he felt happy and contented—until he noticed what was missing.

"Hey, what happened to Miguel?" he demanded.

Chel shrugged. "I don't know."

"Oh my God. He's gone! Miguel's gone! He's loose! What am I going to do? Oh, no!" Tulio's gold clattered to the floor. He charged around the room, looking in every corner—then finally he sank into a couch with a groan. "Ohhhh, no-o-o-o..."

"Miguel is right, you worry too much," Chel said as she walked around behind him. Firmly but gently, she placed her hands on his shoulders and began to massage them.

Her touch was magic. "Ahh," Tulio sighed. "Ooh.

Yeah. Down, down, down...ahh. Ooh..."

Tulio closed his eyes and felt the warmth of her hands, tender but firm. He thought about her beautiful face, about how pleasant it would be to forget the plan and—

Abruptly he leaped to his feet. She was distracting him—and the rule was no slipups, no distractions. "Wow! No! *Biiiiig* trouble! Wow! Look, sweetheart, we're in the middle of a con here, walking the razor's edge. On the one hand, gold. On the other hand, painful, agonizing failure!"

Chel settled on the couch and stretched out her legs.

"I can't afford any temptation—*distractions!*" Chel took his breath away. She was gorgeous. She could spoil everything. He walked behind the couch, trying desperately not to look at her. "So! Uh, I'm sorry. *So* sorry. But perhaps another time, another place, hmm?"

Chel turned and smiled at him over her shoulder. "Too bad. I'm free now."

Those shoulders. They were so...smooth. Just begging to be massaged. Tulio inched closer.

"I'm not really sure I trust you," Tulio said.

"I'm not really asking you to trust me, am I?" Chel asked.

Tulio gulped. What was the harm in a *little* loosening up? It might clear the mind. Besides, he owed her a massage. Fair was fair.

He placed his hands on the back of her shoulders and

began to rub. Chel purred. She turned toward him, eyes closed, lips puckered.

Tulio knew he was in trouble.

At that moment, Miguel was strolling through El Dorado. But he was no longer admiring the splendid architecture and stunning jewels.

He was noticing the strange emptiness in the streets. Only a few guards were out today. As if everyone else were in hiding.

"Excuse me," Miguel called out. "Where is everybody?"

A guard turned and bowed low. "They've been cleared from the streets, my lord, so the city can be cleansed. As you ordered."

"Cleansed?" Miguel asked.

"Yes, so the Age of the Jaguar can begin."

Age of the Jaguar? Before he could ask what *that* meant, scuffling noises broke out from across the plaza. Miguel spun around to see another guard roughing up a citizen.

He ran toward them. "Hey, stop that! Stand back. What are you doing? Stop that!"

The guard turned. His eyes went wide when he saw Miguel, and he bowed low. "Lawbreakers are to be punished severely, my lord."

Miguel scowled at him.

The guard's face fell. Disobeying a god was breaking the law. Instantly he released the man. "As you ordered."

"It seems I've been giving a lot of orders, haven't I?" Miguel remarked.

"Tzekel-Kan has made your commands clear, my lord," the guard replied.

Miguel nodded. So that was it—Tzekel-Kan was giving the orders and claiming they came from the gods. "Here's an order: take the day off!"

As the guard scurried off, Miguel reached out to help the prisoner up. "Are you all right?"

The man looked petrified. Thinking that Miguel required a sacrifice for his kindness, he quickly removed his gold earrings and held them out.

"Oh, no," Miguel said, "it's all right. Please!"

Fear, relief, and confusion played across the man's face as he backed away into a pile of trash. As everything clattered to the ground, he ran off.

Miguel shook his head. Something was definitely wrong. The atmosphere in El Dorado had changed.

Among the fallen trash, he noticed a loom. Picking it up, he tested the tautness of the strings and began strumming it like a guitar—softly at first, to himself.

Out of the corner of his eye, he saw movements—people hidden behind walls and bushes and trees.

Miguel strolled around, strumming louder. With a broad smile, he coaxed frightened townspeople out of hiding. Altivo joined them, wandering over from the temple with a group of boys and girls.

The children were kicking a ball back and forth. With a smile, Miguel set down his guitar and joined them in a pickup game. The crowd, now growing more relaxed, cheered them on.

In all the merriment, no one saw the High Priest hiding among the shadows.

Tzekel-Kan frowned. This was odd. He had never heard of a god playing with mortals like this. He flipped through his sacred codex and found a drawing of a god-like figure playing a game similar to the one Miguel was playing—except that the ball was a skull. And near that image was the face of the Dark God—the powerful, conquering figure who looked neither like Tulio nor Miguel.

What was going on here?

"This is—not what I expected," Tzekel-Kan murmured to himself. "Perhaps Lord Tulio will enlighten me."

Closing the codex, Tzekel-Kan headed for the gods' temple.

"My lord? Excuse me!"

At the sound of Tzekel-Kan's voice, Tulio tried to jump up from behind the couch—but Chel was weighing him down.

"The High Priest!" Chel whispered. "What's he going to think if he finds one of the gods like this with me?"

Tulio shrugged. "'Lucky god'?"

"Hello?" Tzekel-Kan called out.

Chel began to crawl out from behind the couch, out of Tzekel-Kan's field of vision.

Tulio leaped up. "Oh! Tzekel-Kan! What brings you here?"

"I—I humbly request an audience with you, my lord," Tzekel-Kan said with a bow.

"Lord, yes," Tulio replied. "What can I do for you?"

"My lord, I have just seen Lord Miguel out among the people."

Tulio recoiled in mock surprise. "*Really?* Well!"

"Ah, then you're aware of the problem?"

"Oh, for some time now," Tulio said gravely.

"Then, if I may be so bold as to offer some advice…?"

"All right—shoot."

Chel sneaked around Tzekel-Kan and waved to Tulio, making faces as if to say, *Don't listen! Get him out of here!*

"My lord," Tzekel-Kan said, "you are perfect."

Tulio smiled modestly. "Well, go on."

"But in your perfection you cannot know how imperfect humans are. Like snakes, they are spineless and slippery…" With a wave of his arm, he summoned his magic powers. A wisp of smoke appeared, instantly transforming into a snake.

Tulio nearly cried out.

"They are untrustworthy as rats," Tzekel-Kan continued, "stealing and cheating with no remorse…"

With another gesture, he created a pack of rats that swarmed around their feet.

Tulio jumped back in horror.

"…Spinning webs of lies like spiders…"

Enormous spiderwebs appeared out of thin air, strung across the room. As a huge spider crawled across them, Tzekel-Kan grabbed it, crushing it to death in his bare fist.

"Eaaaagh!" Tulio squealed. "Disgusting!"

"They're *beyond* disgusting!" Tzekel-Kan retorted.

"Yeah. Yeah. Way beyond."

"Then we're in agreement?" Tzekel-Kan asked. "I'll begin the necessary preparation immediately. Now, do you prefer your victims bound to an altar? Or do you prefer them free-range?"

Tulio scratched his head. "Tzek, you've lost me."

"My lord, these people will not respect you if they do not fear you."

"And, of course, we'll *make* them fear us," Tulio said, trying desperately to sound tough, "by—"

"Sacrifice!" Tzekel-Kan cut in. "As it is prophesied, the history of the Age of the Jaguar will be written in—"

"Ink?"

"Blood!"

Tulio's skin crawled. Being a god was one thing. Sacrificing people was a different story. "Blood. Of course! Well, this is important stuff, and I really should consult with Lord Miguel right away…about the entire blood issue."

He grabbed Chel's arm and led her down the stairs.

This guy was worse than crazy—he had access to some powerful stuff, and he was dangerous.

Tzekel-Kan beamed as he watched them go. "Finally, we're *connecting*."

Miguel's ball game had grown. It was a sport he'd never played before—a bit like soccer, but the players were mainly hitting the ball with their hips.

Racing after a high, looping fly, Miguel came face-to-face with Tulio.

The ball beaned Tulio on the head. "What do you think you're doing?" he growled.

Miguel backed away. "Um...lying low."

Tulio had no patience for Miguel's nonsense. Tzekel-Kan's little show had spooked him. If the High Priest caught on to their alibi, they were snake food. "Look. Change of plans. We have to grab what we can carry and get out of here—now!"

"Why?" Miguel pleaded.

"Because the High Priest is nuts! He wants—"

"THIS IS UNACCEPTABLE!" The enraged voice of Tzekel-Kan cut off the conversation.

As the townspeople shrank away, Tulio turned to Miguel. "Yeah! Yeah! Like he said!"

"THE GODS SHOULD NOT BE PLAYING BALL LIKE THIS!" Tzekel-Kan thundered, swiftly approaching the area.

"Well, exactly!" Tulio echoed.

With dread, Tulio listened to Tzekel-Kan's command—that the gods should not play against the weak, but against the strongest, cruelest, most skilled athletes in El Dorado.

As he gestured grandly toward the enormous stadium, the citizens let out a gasp of joy and raced for the seats.

ten

TULIO GLARED AT MIGUEL AS THEY APPROACHED THE FIELD.

"Well, don't blame *me*!" Miguel said.

"I blame you," Tulio snarled. He was not going to let Miguel talk his way out of this one.

The citizens swarmed into the stadium from all over. They sat shoulder to shoulder on the marble seats, cheering even before the action had begun.

Altivo whinnied with fear. Even Bibo the armadillo, chasing butterflies among the grass, stopped for a moment to ogle the scene.

Chel swallowed hard. This could end the charade in a moment. Her mind raced, trying to think of a way to save Miguel and Tulio's reputation—but her thoughts came up empty.

Tulio was overwhelmed. He had never seen a field

quite as big as this one. It was completely unmarked—no goals, no lines on the field at all.

He leaned over to Chel. "What is the object of this game, pray tell?"

"You've got to knock the ball through the hoop," she replied.

"What hoop?" Tulio asked.

Chel glanced upward. "That hoop."

High above them, at the top of an imposing stone wall, jutted a thick stone ring.

"That's impossible!" Tulio said. "We're going to lose!"

"Gods don't lose," Chel replied matter-of-factly.

"Heep-ha! *Heep-ha! HEEP-HA!*" The shouts started softly, then grew to a loud, guttural chant.

From behind a wall marched the opposing team.

Miguel's breath caught. Tulio's knees almost gave way. Altivo shied. The men were enormous. With pecs like sides of beef and arms like thickly knotted rope.

"My lords," Tzekel-Kan called out, "Chief Tannabok's warriors are the finest ballplayers in the city—fifteen mere mortals against two gods!"

Tulio and Miguel both felt faint.

"I realize it's a bit uneven," Tzekel-Kan continued, "but I do hope they'll challenge you enough to make the game interesting." Turning to the crowd, he shouted, "Play ball!"

A referee walked toward the center of the field with a large leather ball.

"Crush them into dust," Tzekel-Kan said giddily to Tulio and Miguel.

Crush? Dust? Tulio and Miguel, at that moment, would have rather silenced a volcano.

As the referee threw in the ball, the two friends stood still, legs locked.

The warriors charged. With a sharp *slap*, the ball shot straight for Tulio and Miguel like a bullet.

They did the only thing they could—ducked.

As the ball winged past them, the crowd let out a loud gasp.

Tzekel-Kan looked baffled. "My lords, were you not supposed to put the ball into play?"

Tulio bolted to his feet. "Oh, well, no. We were merely demonstrating the, uh, traditional, uh, first-avoidance maneuver."

"Ah," Tzekel-Kan said with puzzled politeness. "I have never heard of such a thing."

"Excuse me?" Miguel said haughtily. "*Who* invented this game?"

Tzekel-Kan's face reddened. "Why, the gods, of course."

Chief Tannabok smiled at the rebuke.

Miguel picked up the ball and turned confidently toward the field.

"I'm warning you," Tulio said to him, "don't push your luck with this guy Tzekel-Kan."

"But Tulio," Miguel said, "we're the gods."

He threw the ball in play. It shot from player to player, bounding off their rocklike hips. They thundered up the field, dodging and weaving.

This time Miguel and Tulio chased after them.

Thwock!

One of the warriors sent the ball flying. It rose upward and sailed through the hoop—easy point for the mortals.

This was no contest. Tulio saw the whole scheme falling to pieces. "This is impossible!" he exclaimed.

The sound of the crowd was deafening. They wanted action.

Miguel threw the ball back into play.

Thwock! Thwock-thwock-thwock-thwock!

All Miguel and Tulio could do was watch the ball. The warriors' second basket was easier than the first. It was two to nothing.

"Tulio!" Chel screamed. "Use your hip!"

Bibo was asleep at her feet now, curled up into a ball. She lifted him in one hand and slammed him against her side to demonstrate the proper technique. Bibo squealed with surprise. "The *hip*!" Chel repeated.

Miguel and Tulio lunged desperately for the ball.

"HEE-HA! HEE-HA!" the players chanted, battering the two men as if they were rag dolls.

Disbelief and distress swept across the stands like a chilling wind. Chel turned away in horror, dropping Bibo. Woozy, the armadillo climbed into a basket full of game balls to rest.

Finally Miguel got hold of the ball and began running, joined quickly by Tulio. The field, miraculously, was open.

But Chel was aghast. "The other way!" she shouted,

pointing them to the correct goal. "The other way!"

Tulio and Miguel skidded to a stop, finally realizing they were going the wrong way, but it was too late. They were instantly buried under a pile of players. One of them elbowed Miguel in the face.

"Foul!" Chel cried. "That was a foul!"

The referee said nothing. "Mortals Fouling Gods" was not in the rule books.

"HEE-HA! HEE-HA!"

Play continued and the score climbed: three to zero... four to zero.

Five...six...Soon Chel lost count. She could only turn away, cringing, seeing her own plans, her own escape, evaporate into smoke.

Thud.

The ball landed out of bounds, in the basket of balls near Chel.

"New ball! New ball!" one of the players shouted.

She reached down—and almost grabbed hold of Bibo. All curled up, he looked just like a ball.

The idea had occurred to him, too. He gave her a sly wink.

Tulio and Miguel staggered toward them. Nearly out of breath, Tulio pleaded, "How long does this last, anyway?"

Chel pointed to a line at the far end of the field. "The game is over when the shadow touches this line."

The sun was setting. Its shadow reached across most

of the field. Only a few feet of light remained before the line was in darkness.

"We need a miracle," Miguel moaned.

"No," Tulio replied in a rueful voice, "we need to cheat."

Chel smiled. She handed him a new ball.

A ball that blinked.

Tulio and Miguel grinned. Bibo was perfect. And he was on their side.

They raced back onto the field, bouncing the armadillo between them, hip to hip. Bibo used his own strength to hurtle through the air at blinding speed. He stuck with Tulio and Miguel, veering around, over, and under the opponents.

Trying to follow, the players lurched left and right. They smacked into each other, falling to the ground.

Tulio and Miguel cut a clear path to the hoop, and—

Whoosh!

Bibo shot clear through. Goal for the gods!

"WOOOOOH!" screamed Chel.

The crowd was on its feet, stamping and shouting as Miguel and Tulio quickly gained possession again. They darted up the field. Bibo was fine-tuned now, bouncing between them with pinpoint accuracy.

The warriors were ready. Concentrating fiercely, they raced after the ball.

Bibo veered away. Miguel and Tulio ducked.

Crack. Mooff. Ugggh.

Two by two the players collided in midair, leaving a trail of fallen bodies. Miguel and Tulio passed Bibo straight upward—and when he came down, they hipped him from both sides.

Bibo squirted toward Altivo, who batted him up and through the hoop.

The crowd thundered approval. Miguel danced for joy, whooping and laughing. "Who's the god?" he shouted.

"*You* the god!" Tulio said.

"No, *you* the god!"

"No, *you* the god. Fine."

Time was wasting. The shadow signaling the end of the game was drawing nearer. Tulio and Miguel grabbed Bibo and headed into the field again.

The players no longer looked so big and bad. Bruised and battered was more like it.

But they were not about to give up. Far from it. With grim determination, one of them grabbed hold of Bibo and hipped him toward the hoop.

At the last moment, Bibo puffed out his chest.

Splat.

He bounced back, too big to fit through.

Miguel grabbed the rebound. He and Tulio maneuvered back to the hoop, dancing, spinning, hitting the ball from behind.

Bibo kept his eye on the hoop, correcting Tulio and Miguel's aim, maneuvering in midair…

Goal.

Twisting…

Goal.

Sliding...

Goal.

Rolling...

Goal.

Goal.

Goal.

As the shadow drew to within an inch of the line, Bibo sailed through to tie the game.

He bounced out of bounds and landed in the ball basket, his head spinning.

Chel was screaming. Jumping. Behind her, the spectators rocked the stadium.

Tulio and Miguel climbed onto Altivo. If they were going to win this, they wanted to do it in *style*. On their horse.

Chel reached into the basket and threw the ball back to Tulio and Miguel.

Altivo galloped forward. The warriors gathered under the hoop, ready to do anything to win the game.

Miguel and Tulio hit the ball between them, circling in for the final shot, teasing the crowd, waiting for the shadow to close the gap.

"Tssssss!" Chel hissed from the sidelines.

Her face was ashen as she held up a beaten and bedraggled object—Bibo.

Miguel and Tulio nearly fell off Altivo. They were playing with a ball, a *real* ball.

The hoop loomed closer. Their opponents surrounded

them, suddenly looking more fearsome than ever.

Tulio whacked at the ball with his fist, but only nicked it. It rose feebly upward.

Miguel knew it would never make it all the way. He rose up on Altivo and jumped—but the ball was out of reach.

As he fell back, he kicked out desperately.

Thwap.

He made contact with his foot. The ball lofted toward the hoop.

Miguel tumbled into Tulio, and both men fell to the field. They watched, holding their breaths. Around them, all noise ceased.

With a soft thump, the ball landed inside the hoop.

But it didn't emerge from the other side. It stayed there—balanced on the inner rim, motionless.

Slowly the shadow approached the line.

eleven

IT WAS ONLY A MOMENT, BUT IT SEEMED LIKE AN ETERNITY TO ALTIVO. As he stood beneath the hoop, he noticed that all eyes were fixed on the ball. No one was watching him.

Instinctively he lifted his hoof and gave the wall a quick, firm kick.

The wall shook briefly. Inside the hoop, the ball teetered.

It paused at the edge for a long moment—and then dropped through.

"HOOORRAAAHHHHHH!"

The citizens leaped out of their seats with a joyful roar.

"I *love* this game!" Tzekel-Kan cried out.

"Yyyyyessss!" cried Tulio and Miguel, running toward a deliriously cheering Chel.

Tulio picked her up and whirled her around. "Well done, partner!" he said.

The High Priest strode toward them with Chief Tannabok. Both men beamed proudly.

"My lords, congratulations on your victory," Tzekel-Kan said. "And now you will, of course, wish to have the losing team *sacrificed* to your glory."

The players dropped to their knees. Their eyes rose to Tulio and Miguel, wide and frightened, as the boisterous crowd instantly hushed.

"Not again," Miguel said. "Look, Tzekel-Kan—"

Tulio nudged him. As far as he was concerned, this was El Dorado's problem. They could decide what to do—after Tulio and Miguel were gone. "Uh, Miguel…?"

"Forget the sacrifices!" Miguel barreled on.

"*Miguel!*" Tulio said sternly.

"We don't want any sacrifices!"

Tzekel-Kan began to protest, "But the sacred writings say that you will devour the wicked and the unrighteous—"

"Well, I don't see anyone here who fits that description," Miguel retorted.

Tulio's heart dropped. Miguel was crossing Tzekel-Kan. Bad idea. Very bad.

"As Speaker for the Gods," Tzekel-Kan said tensely, "it would be my privilege to point them out."

"The gods are speaking for themselves now! This city and these people have no need for you anymore!" Ignoring Tulio's protests, Miguel elbowed past Tzekel-

Kan and gestured for the players to rise. He'd had enough of this. "There will be no sacrifices. Not now, not ever. Now get out!"

Tzekel-Kan recoiled. This was not in his plan—it was an outrage to the sacred signs. The god's behavior was unimaginable.

A noise began in the stands, slowly growing into a cheer that was as loud as any in the game.

The warriors stood, smiling gratefully at Miguel. Not one of them feared the High Priest now.

But Tzekel-Kan did not care. His eyes had focused on Miguel's forehead, at the sight of something he had not expected to see—a drop of blood.

He backed away, his voice a sinister grumble. "As the…*gods*…command."

Behind him the stands were emptying. The citizens swarmed onto the field, rushing toward Tulio and Miguel.

Tulio tried to pull his friend away, but Miguel turned toward the crowd, arms open. "Not bad for my first commandment," he exclaimed with pride.

"*Miguel…*" Tulio said sharply. "*The little voice?*"

No one paid Tzekel-Kan much attention as he sneaked out the back of the throng. No one saw him rush away.

But as he entered his temple, his acolyte nearly fell over. He had never seen his master in such a good mood.

"Do you know why the gods demand blood?" Tzekel-Kan blurted out.

"I don't know," the acolyte answered.

"Because *gods don't bleed*!" As Tzekel-Kan paced the temple floor, he began flipping through his codex. "There are dark magics here…and power…and—oh. Oh, my. My, my, my." He stopped short, his mouth tightening into a gruesome excuse for a grin. "It's not called the Age of the Jaguar for nothing."

He looked out over the city—at the happy citizens coursing through the streets, at the dock laborers building Tulio and Miguel's exquisite boat.

"This," Tzekel-Kan said, "will be a delightful way to bid the false gods good-bye!"

As he burst into a fierce cackle, his acolyte stared dumbly. He had no idea what was so funny.

But he laughed anyway, to make the High Priest happy.

That was his job.

Three days—that was how long it would take to build Tulio and Miguel's boat.

The gods' boat.

No one in El Dorado doubted their divinity now. In the chief's boatyard, workers toiled day and night, chanting happily, pleased to be devoting their skills to the two kind and powerful deities. On the streets, the citizens greeted Miguel and Tulio with gifts of flowers, food, and drink. A blacksmith fitted Altivo with horseshoes of solid gold. Sculptors created statues of the gods and artists painted their likenesses. A portrait of their winning goal was carved onto a monument. No corner of the city was left without an image of Tulio and Miguel.

Now that Tzekel-Kan had retreated quietly to his temple, Tulio was lightening up. Chel coaxed him into telling stories about Spain. Swept up in the memories, he broke into a demonstration of flamenco dancing—stamping, wailing, scowling, moving his arms in precise arcs.

She nearly died laughing.

On the evening of the second day, Miguel walked along the hull of the boat. It was already near completion, the workers polishing furiously and putting on the finishing touches. In one more day, he'd be saying good-bye forever to paradise—and godhood.

The thought made Miguel's heart sink. He loved the city of gold. Its hidden wonders, its hard-working and high-spirited people who loved and revered him—it was all he could ever want.

Chief Tannabok followed close behind, proudly admiring the handiwork. The boat was sturdy and grand, colorful and crafted with love.

Like all of El Dorado.

Miguel nodded distractedly, pretending to inspect the boat. If he could find fault, if he could stall long enough, perhaps he wouldn't have to go....

"Well," he said, "it's...nice."

"Nice?" Chief Tannabok repeated warily.

"Yes, it's nice, but...is it really fit for the gods?"

The chief looked devastated. "My lord?"

"I have been around boats, believe me, and that—"

Miguel groped for something—*anything* to pick on. "Uh…the pointy, tall…that—uh, *thing*, the long, up-and-down thing—"

"Mast?" Chief Tannabok asked tentatively, wondering if Miguel was testing his knowledge of sailing terms.

"Mast! Look at it! There's not nearly enough…*rope*."

"Rope?"

"Yes, rope. Exactly my point. Vertical ascension requires a lot more rope. And look at this—this doesn't look at all secure!" He grabbed a railing and shook it hard, but it didn't budge. "Chief, I'm sorry, I'm sorry, but…all in all, it's a complete do-over."

Chief Tannabok gave him a level, appraising look. "You know, Lord Miguel, if you wish to stay, you only need to say so."

Miguel brightened. "You mean, forever?"

"Of course!"

"Oh, no, I can't," Miguel said, snapping back to reality. The plan—he had to remember the plan. "I have to go back with Tulio. We're partners."

"Big plans in the other world, huh?" the chief asked with a good-natured smile.

"Yup, big plans," Miguel said with new resolve. As tempting as a new life in El Dorado might be, he could never abandon Tulio.

The chief gave Miguel a wry look, then turned to go. "Well, then, I'd better go get some more rope."

"Uh, chief? Um, forget about the rope. My mistake."

The chief shrugged and smiled gently. "To err is human."

Exactly, Miguel thought.

But as he began walking back toward the temple, he stopped. Chief Tannabok's words echoed in his mind. The chief was a smart man, one of the wisest he'd ever met.

Did he suspect?

Miguel looked back over his shoulder, but the chief had turned away.

At the gods' temple, Tulio lugged an armful of coins and trinkets out of the storage room. It was time to divvy up the gold.

Chel stood among three piles of it, two small and one large. She pointed Tulio to the bigger pile. "That goes over there."

Tulio started to put it down but stopped halfway. "Uh, Chel? What are we doing?"

"Dividing up the gold," Chel replied. "Half for you and Miguel, half for me."

"Half? But I thought we were..." Tulio firmly set down his load. He was wise to her tricks. No one cheated him out of gold. Not even Chel. "Oh, I see....I'll tell you what. I'll let you come back to Spain with us like you wanted, and, um...yeah, I could see my way to throwing you... ten percent."

Chel eyed him coolly. "You know, maybe I *won't* go to

Spain with you, and I'll take a third."

"Oh. Like you don't *want to* go to Spain."

"Oh. Like you don't want me to go to Spain."

Tulio shrugged. "I want you to want…"

"Mm-hm?"

"…What you want."

"Mm-hm. Go on."

Tulio exhaled. He owed Chel the truth. She deserved to know how he felt about her—if she hadn't figured it out already. "All right. Cards on the table. I want you to come to Spain with me and Miguel. Mostly me."

Chel waited…

"Especially me," Tulio continued sheepishly.

And waited…

"*Only* me. Forget Miguel." With a shy, pleading smile, Tulio took her hand. "Okay, deal?"

"Deal," Chel replied.

Tulio was overjoyed. He couldn't believe his good fortune. Finally he had what he wanted. The gold. The girl. Soon he'd be back home, where he could live *right* for a change—rich and happy, with Miguel as his partner and the woman of his dreams by his side.

As he looked into Chel's deeply brown eyes, he imagined seeing in them the reflection of the Spanish sun. He pictured standing with her on the sandy coast outside their villa—no, their *castle*. It would be next door to Miguel's, of course, the two grandest estates in the land.

He leaned toward Chel and felt the sun's warmth against her face. Chel lifted her arms and wrapped them lovingly around Tulio as they enjoyed a long, luxurious kiss.

Wrapped in their own world, they did not see the shadow in the entryway.

And they could not have imagined the pain on the face that watched them.

Miguel's face.

As his shock slowly gave way to heartache, Miguel backed away. Tulio's words were etched in his brain:

Forget Miguel.

It was the last thing he ever expected his friend to say. He slumped past Altivo, who stared open-jawed at the couple.

Miguel's mind reeled. He was about to leave El Dorado. He was about to give up the life of a god in the most wondrous place he'd ever seen, a place that surpassed his grandest dreams—and for what?

For the partnership—everything was for the partnership. Miguel and Tulio, Tulio and Miguel, together always, no matter what. Despite all his dreaminess, all his straying, Miguel had never questioned this agreement. Ever.

But now it felt hollow and meaningless. A partnership was two-sided. It had rules, too—like honesty and loyalty. Without those things, it might as well be dead.

Betrayal hurt. It hurt deeper than he'd imagined. But it could be two-sided, also.

"Okay, forget Tulio," Miguel said with a heavy sigh, pulling on Altivo's bridle.

With a sympathetic nod, and a final helpless glance back toward the temple, Altivo followed.

twelve

AS NIGHT SETTLED OUTSIDE THE TEMPLE OF THE HIGH PRIEST, Tzekel-Kan's acolyte stirred a bubbling, greenish liquid in a thick vat.

"Well?" Tzekel-Kan demanded. "Is it ready yet?"

The acolyte gave the liquid a hard look. He grabbed a cup from a shelf, dipped it into the vat, and held out a sample for the High Priest to taste.

Tzekel-Kan glared at him.

The acolyte cringed. Procedure must be followed. He squeezed in a little lime and topped the drink with a tiny bamboo umbrella.

Now Tzekel-Kan took it. Bringing it to his lips, he took a tiny sip.

His eyes bulged. His face turned red. His hair stood on end. The codex fell to the floor.

Catching his breath, Tzekel-Kan thought a moment.

It was powerful—but was it enough? "It seems to be missing something," he murmured.

He tried to focus, but his eyes were playing tricks. As he looked at the codex, the images began to move. The prophecies swirled around each other, fading and brightening—until finally Tzekel-Kan saw an image of the acolyte, kneeling in front of the brew.

A sign.

"Ah, that's it!" Tzekel-Kan said. "It needs more... *body*."

With a swift kick, he sent the acolyte into the vat. He chortled as the young man disappeared, screaming, into the green brew.

Smoke began swirling over the vat, gathering into a dense cloud...

KA-BOOOOM!

Tzekel-Kan staggered back. He sheltered his eyes from the eruption of light. Around him, objects vibrated as if electrified. A glowing green current shot through his body, charging it with mystical power. It connected him with the statue of the stone jaguar, crouching in the corner.

Slowly the statue began to move.

That evening, the entire city turned out for a last banquet for the gods.

Tulio sat forward on his throne, stuffing his face, waving at the citizens, happy that his plan had worked.

Miguel tried to smile, but he couldn't. He tried to eat,

but he had no appetite. Part of him wanted to rage at Tulio. Part of him wanted to plead *why?*

But he remained silent, stymied by the rush of feelings.

Suddenly a group of native children raced into the plaza and announced a pageant.

Imitating Miguel, a boy strutted in front of the other children, shouting, "The gods deserve a proper tribute! Stop! There will be no more sacrifices. Not now. Not ever!"

Tulio chuckled and leaned toward Miguel. "That kid does you better than you do you! Some send-off, huh? We're finally at the go-back-to-Spain-and-live-like-kings part." Seeing Chel and Altivo make their way through the crowd, he waved.

"Well," Miguel said bitterly, "isn't 'king' kind of a step down from 'god'?"

"What?" Tulio gave his partner a shrewd look. He could tell Miguel was having second thoughts about leaving. "Hey, Miguel, we can't stay here. We have a plan, remember?"

Miguel's eyes were cold. "Nobody said *you* have to stay."

"Whaaa—?" Tulio hadn't expected *that*. He felt as if he'd been punched. Split up the team? The thought had never crossed his mind. All along, everything had been *we*. In Spain and in El Dorado. Tulio could barely remember when it was any other way. Sure, the gold would be nice—and sure, he was in love with Chel. But a life without Miguel? It wouldn't be right. "But—"

Before he could answer, a horrific noise thundered across the land—a noise that sounded as if it arose from the earth itself.

Miguel and Tulio screamed. The children scattered, shrieking.

Tzekel-Kan stood at the door of his temple. Beside him, a shadow emerged. Its footprints landed hard and loud, shaking the ground, like boulders dropping from the sky.

Out of the darkness beamed two eyes, piercing green— the green of the potion that bubbled within the temple.

Slowly the stone jaguar descended the stairs.

"*Now,*" Tzekel-Kan shouted, "*everyone will know the truth of your divinity!*"

thirteen

"LORD MIGUEL! Help us!"

"Save us!"

"Lord Tulio-o-o!"

The cries rang out as the jaguar stormed through the city. With stealth and speed it hunted down citizens, crushing them underfoot. It heaved its green stone flanks against the jeweled buildings, pulverizing them. No weapon could pierce its hide, no strategy could divert it—and nothing in its path survived.

Miguel and Tulio huddled frightened behind a wall. They had never felt less godlike. Each citizen's cry that reached their ears felt like a stab wound. They wanted to help the people of El Dorado—*their* people—but they were helpless.

"HAAAAA-HAHAHA!" Tzekel-Kan's laughter resounded

throughout the city, mocking Tulio and Miguel.

But suddenly among the sounds of devastation came the rhythm of approaching hoofbeats. Tulio and Miguel looked behind them. With relief, they saw Altivo, driven by Chel.

"Come on, get on!" Chel urged.

The two men scrambled onto the horse and Tulio quickly took the reins. With a loud, *"Altivo! Ya!"* he spurred the mighty warhorse onward, away from the path of the monster.

Not far away, at the top of the temple stairs, Tzekel-Kan stood expressionless. He saw all—but not through his own eyes. The potion had changed him. The dark magic had taken effect.

Tzekel-Kan saw through the eyes of the jaguar. He felt what the jaguar felt.

And both wanted revenge on the impostor gods.

The monster bounded toward Tulio and Miguel, cutting off their escape path. Altivo bolted up a nearby staircase—but the jaguar followed, taking the stairs three at a time...four...

Altivo screamed in fright. He kicked with his rear leg. *CRUUNCCCCH!*

A dead hit—in the center of the jaguar's eye.

The monster bellowed with pain—and high above the temple, Tzekel-Kan echoed his cry, writhing.

With a swipe of his paw, the stone creature struck Altivo. Chel flew off one side, Tulio and Miguel the other.

"*Tulio*!" Chel shouted.

The jaguar's ears perked up at the cry. It turned, training its good eye on Chel.

Quickly Miguel and Tulio grabbed pieces of the broken stone stairway and threw them. "Hey, you big pussycat!" Tulio taunted.

The jaguar swung around. Its teeth were bared, its gaze murderous.

"Altivo!" Tulio yelled. "Get Chel out of here!"

The horse sped toward Chel. She reached up, grabbing his mane, and pulled herself onto his back.

Tulio and Miguel raced away. The jaguar leaped after them, snarling furiously. It struck with its paw, missing by inches.

The two men felt the wind at their backs, searing hot. They ducked away, through a narrow passageway and out of the city.

A lava field stretched out before them, gray, flat, and parched. Through cracks in the thin, hardened crust, molten lava glowed red hot. As their footsteps thudded hollowly against the surface, they felt the heat through the soles of their sandals.

The jaguar pounced...

CRRACKK!

The force of its landing sent a ripple through the field. Molten lava spat upward like liquid fire. Miguel and Tulio leaped away.

The jaguar plunged through the surface and into the hot magma. It roared in agony, trying to claw its way upward, but lava weighed its body down, melting its paws into misshapen stumps.

"Move!" Tulio shouted. "Move! Jump!"

Miguel and Tulio ran back, clambering over the struggling beast toward safer ground. They collapsed on firm soil, safely away from the field.

Screaming hideously, the monster sank. Tulio and Miguel watched it disappear into the molten sea.

"Are you OK?" Tulio said, catching his breath.

"Oh, I'm fine," Miguel said sharply. "This is such fun!"

RRRRAAGGHHHH!

The earth erupted in a shower of orange-red. Snarling, the jaguar rose from the depths.

Its cold green eye now stared out from a steaming, liquefied mass. Its body was gruesomely distorted from the lava and the heat.

But it was alive. And angry.

And airborne.

Tulio and Miguel ran away, back into the darkness of the city. But the jaguar landed right behind them.

They stopped short. Below them, the ground ended. Beyond it was bottomless blackness. They knew where they were now—on the ledge overlooking the ceynote well. The jaguar was stalking toward them. And they had nowhere to go but down.

"I know what you are!" boomed the voice of Tzekel-Kan as he strode out of the night, keeping the jaguar at bay. "And I know what you are not. And you are not gods!"

Tulio's mind reached desperately back for a plan of escape—back into his history of scrapes with Miguel. Suddenly an idea struck him. It was crazy but it had worked before. He looked at Miguel in mock horror. "You're not a god? You lied to me? How dare you!"

"Hey," he said to Tzekel-Kan, "it was *his* stupid plan."

Tzekel-Kan looked confused. "Oh?"

"My plan was that we should lie low!" Tulio said. "But *your* plan was to run off and be all, 'Oh, look at me, look at me, I'm a god!'"

"That's not true!" Miguel protested.

"No? Who are you kidding? You're buying your own con! Listen, Mr. High-and-Mighty, we'd both be sailing out of here with a mountain of gold if you had just listened to me!"

Tzekel-Kan smiled. This was amusing. This would make their demise easier—and more fun.

"Well, now *you've* got all the precious gold," Miguel said. "*And* Chel! So what do you need *me* for?"

"Maybe I *don't* need you anymore!" Tulio shot back.

"Then why don't you just go back to Spain and I'll stay here—and we'll both get what we want!"

"That's fine with me, pal!"

Miguel slapped Tulio. "Fine with me, too!"

"Ooh!" Tzekel-Kan squealed with joy at the prospect of violence.

Tulio slapped Miguel back. "Fine!"

"Ouch!" Tzekel-Kan said gleefully.

"Okay!" Miguel cried out.

"*Allll riiiiiight!*" Tulio and Miguel shouted together, suddenly whirling toward Tzekel-Kan—and landing a solid double punch in the jaw.

With a grunt of surprise, Tzekel-Kan lurched backward and fell to the ground.

"Tie him up!" Tulio lunged for a tangle of vines, hanging from a tree.

Miguel grabbed a vine, too—but they were both too late. Tzekel-Kan was rising to his feet, his face dark and vengeful. He growled with rage.

A deep, bone-shaking growl answered him.

The jaguar.

They'd forgotten the jaguar.

With catlike reflexes, it leaped from behind Tzekel-Kan, straight for Tulio and Miguel!

They leaped away—and plunged into the well.

fourteen

"WHO-O-O-O-OA!"

Tulio's fingers were still clutching the vine. It pulled taut. His body banged against the wall of the well.

He was hanging from the vine, safe and alive.

He caught sight of Miguel's silhouette nearby, dangling, holding tight to his vine too.

Above them, the jaguar descended sharply. Too sharply. Heavy with molten lava, it landed hard—smack on top of Tzekel-Kan.

In a shower of soil and roots and rock, the ledge broke off.

"*AAAAGGHH!*" Tzekel-Kan's scream rang out as he and the jaguar plunged helplessly into the darkness.

Tulio and Miguel watched the two figures fall. As the echoes died, the ceynote well settled into an eerie silence.

They yanked sharply on the vines, climbing upward. They could hear footsteps running toward the well from all sides.

As Miguel reached the top, a crowd gazed over the edge in amazement. At the sight of the surviving gods, they began to roar. Deliriously.

They'd heard Tzekel-Kan's scream. They knew he was gone. They knew they were safe from the stone jaguar—thanks to the gods. As they pulled Miguel up, they wrapped him in hugs, kissing him and slapping him on the back.

"Hey! A little help here, please?" Tulio yelled, still struggling for a foothold.

Chel leaned over the edge and reached down.

Tulio grabbed her hand and pulled. As he emerged over the rim, he saw Miguel fighting his way toward the edge of the crowd, where the chief stood.

"Chief Tanni!" Miguel cried over the cheering, "I've decided to stay!"

"This is wonderful news!" the chief exclaimed. Turning to the crowd, he announced: "What a glorious day for El Dorado—Lord Miguel has decided to live among us!"

The crowd bellowed its approval, carrying Miguel away on its shoulders.

Tulio stood motionless, his face pale.

Miguel had been serious about splitting up. Dead serious.

It didn't make sense. Not after the most thrilling

adventure of their lives. Not after they'd pulled together in classic style—working as one, partners to the end.

This was not the man Tulio knew. *That* Miguel loved danger and excitement—and valued friendship above all.

This Miguel had turned his back on Tulio. Thrown him aside for the life of a false god. No discussion, nothing. As if the friendship never counted.

"Tulio! Is everything okay?" Chel asked.

"Everything is fine," Tulio replied softly, turning away so she couldn't see the expression on his face.

Under the great ceynote well, water rushed in a furious current. It flowed, unseen, below the jungle.

And it finally emerged at the great waterfall, near the entrance to El Dorado. There, Tzekel-Kan tumbled onto the banks, breathless and dazed.

Seeing him, a sentry hid in the bushes and watched. He was wary of the evil High Priest. And he had also heard a band of approaching strangers—the army of Hernan Cortes.

At that moment, Cortes emerged from the jungle. Spotting Tzekel-Kan, he drew out his musket and stepped forward. The High Priest cringed in fear as Cortes dug the barrel behind Tzekel-Kan's ear.

His gold earrings glinted in the light of the rising sun.

"Where did you get these?" Cortes demanded.

Tzekel-Kan now recognized the fearsome figure looming above him. It was the conquering Dark God, whose approach was prophesied in the codex.

An evil smile crept across Tzekel-Kan's face. He was back in business.

As dawn broke, Tulio went through the rooms of the temple, making sure to pack all his things. Departure day had arrived, the day he'd been looking forward to—but he felt no joy. None at all.

His heart had hardened against the friend who had betrayed him. He scowled at Miguel, who was now primping in the mirror, dressed in his best finery. Oddly enough, Miguel looked a little sad.

As far as Tulio was concerned, that served him right. What was he going to do now—make "the face"? Try to convince Tulio that it was all right to destroy a friendship?

Hah. No way.

Miguel watched him go. He couldn't understand why Tulio looked so enraged. Tulio was the one who had what he wanted. Tulio was the one determined to "forget Miguel" and throw away the partnership. Was he going to stand there and let the traitor throw a fit at *him*?

Hah. No way.

Tulio spun around. He was holding the map—the one they'd used to find this place. With an angry thrust, he ripped it in half.

Miguel stiffened. Tulio had stepped over the line. Two could play this game. Turning nonchalantly away, Miguel stuck out his foot and—oops, what a pity, there went a gold statue of Tulio, *plop*, on the floor.

Tulio picked up their game-winning ball and threw it at his ex-friend.

Miguel ducked. The ball ricocheted.

Bonk. It beaned Tulio on the head.

Tulio staggered away. Enough. Time to forget treacherous Miguel and return to Spain. Chin high, he walked out of the temple, descending the right side of the stairs.

Miguel followed, taking the left.

The citizens of El Dorado had gathered at the bottom with Chief Tannabok, to bid Tulio and Chel farewell. Chel stood by Altivo's side at the dock. Bibo scampered between the horse's legs.

With a sad smile, the chief pulled Tulio into an embrace. Miguel hugged Chel good-bye.

Then Tulio walked over to the ball warriors, who stood together, dwarfing everyone else in the crowd. They gave him friendly slaps on the back. The impact nearly knocked him out. As he staggered back, he reached out to pat Altivo on the nose—but the horse gave him a big, slurpy lick on the face.

Any other time, Tulio would have cried out in disgust. This time, he gave in and hugged Altivo good-bye.

When he turned away, he came face to face with Miguel.

"Well, good luck," Miguel said uncertainly.

Tulio nodded. "Yeah, you too."

They shook hands. For a moment they stood there stiffly, their anger in abeyance, fingers still clenched.

Each had a million unfinished thoughts, a sea of unsaid words.

But neither spoke up. What was done was done.

Turning away, Tulio boarded the boat with Chel. As Bibo scampered in after them, Tulio reached for the tie-line, to release it from the dock.

Unseen by all but Altivo, a puff of black smoke arose on the horizon, over the canopy of trees. The horse's ears picked up the faint, distant sound of a gunshot... and another....He began to paw the ground nervously.

"Whoa, boy, what is it? What?" Miguel asked, his eyes following the horse's glance to the distant gunsmoke. Immediately he sensed what it meant. "Cortes," he murmured.

Altivo whinnied and reared up.

"My lord," Chief Tannabok said, "what is it?"

Suddenly the sentry from the waterfall raced toward the chief, his eyes wide with panic. "Chief Tanni! Chief Tanni! Approaching the city is an army of strangers!"

"We are safe here," the chief said reassuringly. "There's only one entrance to the city, and they are never going to find it."

"But, sire," the sentry insisted, "they are being led by Tzekel-Kan!"

The color drained from the chief's face. "He survived?" Quickly turning toward the townspeople, he called out, "Warriors! Prepare yourselves for battle!"

"But, Chief," Miguel said, "they've got weapons of

thunder and lightning, of terrible destruction! You cannot fight them!"

"Then how can we stop them?" the chief asked.

Tulio had been listening to it all. As always, his mind was already working on a plan. Now he had two goals: escape for himself and Chel, and safety for the people of El Dorado. From the boat, he called out, "One moment, please!"

He put his arm around Chel and turned toward a table laden with food for the journey. Bibo was already rummaging through, drinking from a sturdy, cylindrical cup. Tulio grabbed some fruit and began setting it up, like a battle plan. "Okay…here's the gate…here's the boat…"

"Uh-huh?" Chel said. "And?"

Tulio thought a moment. "Here's the gate."

"OK."

"Here's the boat…"

Chel rolled her eyes. "Got that. And?"

"Well…here's the goat and here's the bait…"

Chel began slapping Tulio on the forehead hard—Miguel's old trick. Bibo jumped at the sound. His cup spilled, washing Tulio's "boat" across the table. It turned sideways and crashed against two bananas.

Tulio watched the scene in amazement. He could do it—escape El Dorado and at the same time seal the city off from Cortes. "That's it!" he cried out. "We'll crash the boat into the pillars!"

"That's it?" Chel asked. "But what about the gold?"

Perhaps the plan could be altered a bit. The citizens could topple the pillars, the ones that held the cisterns. But his boat would have to knock over the pillars at the other end of the tunnel, at the waterfall.

The boat would be destroyed, the gold sacrificed, but there was no other way. The thought brought tears to Tulio's eyes.

He got a grip on himself and faced the chief. "I've got a plan..." he announced firmly.

The warriors were swift. And crafty. They constructed a battering ram and collected long ropes. At the river's entrance to El Dorado, they tied the ropes around one of the enormous cisterns, full of water, that stood on either side. Drawing the ropes to the opposite dock, they held taut.

Timing was crucial. The cistern was heavy, poised on short pillars. The mightiest warriors would use the battering ram to knock out those pillars, weakening the support. The people with the ropes would try to guide the fall of the cistern. The procedure would take some time, even with the muscle power of dozens—but if they started now, the cistern would topple just after Tulio and Chel sailed through the gate.

Then the entrance would be sealed forever. El Dorado would be safe. The citizens would be forever cut off from the rest of the world.

And so would Miguel.

Tulio glanced over his shoulder. Miguel was dressed in

Eagle finery, with a robe that resembled folded wings. He looked regal, godly. As if he belonged.

Tulio felt a catch in his throat. Quickly he looked away. There was no time to think of this. No time to imagine life without his best friend.

Survival was all.

Slowly the boat floated toward the gate. Tulio prepared to unfurl the sail. Soon the boat would be speeding away. "Okay, Chief," he called out, eyeing the cistern, calculating the timing. "On my signal...ready? *Hit the pillars!*"

The warriors pushed the battering ram forward. With a loud report, it smashed against a pillar. The cistern vibrated.

They withdrew and lunged again. One pillar broke, and another cracked—and now the cistern began to tip.

But the boat was moving slowly—too slowly. They wouldn't make it at this rate.

"They're breaking too fast!" Tulio shouted.

"Tulio," Chel cried out, "the sail!"

He glanced up. The sail was jammed. A length of rope was twisted around it, preventing it from opening.

He ran to the mast. What now?

Grabbing the mast, he began to climb. He reached out to the sail, trying desperately to untangle the sheeting.

On the dock, Miguel stared at the impending catastrophe.

His heart raced. Tulio's life was in danger. Again. As it

had been against the jaguar. And in the jungle. And on the sea. And in Spain.

Tulio had survived all those dangers. He was a strong, smart man. But this time was different. This time, Miguel was not with him.

Miguel watched Tulio slowly climb up the mast. This was madness—Tulio would never untangle the sail in time. At his angle, he wouldn't have the leverage. And now the ship was almost under the cistern. Tulio and Chel would either be blocked in—or they'd be crushed.

That was something Miguel simply couldn't watch. "They're not going to make it," he cried out. "*Altivo!*"

The warhorse raced up beside him. Miguel jumped on, kicking his heels into the horse's flank. Altivo broke into a dead run along the edge of the water.

Tulio was fumbling with the knot. Below him, Chel shouted frantically. On the shore, the battering ram was still. The warriors—along with Chief Tannabok and scores of citizens—pulled hard on the ropes, trying to keep the cistern upright.

With a sickening sound of falling rock, the cistern tilted slowly downward.

fifteen

TULIO HEARD HOOFBEATS ON THE DOCK. He glanced toward the sound. It was Altivo, his mane blowing in the wind—with Miguel on his back.

With a mighty push, the great warhorse sprang. He soared high over the water toward the boat.

Chel screamed in astonishment. Bibo curled up into a ball.

"Are you crazy?" Tulio yelled.

In midair, Miguel leaped off the horse's back. He sailed through the air, his robe billowing out behind him like an eagle's wings.

Tulio gasped. Miguel seemed to be flying.

Altivo landed on deck with a loud thud. High above, Miguel reached out with his arms. He caught the edge of the sail and swung.

The sail snapped outward, released from the rope. It caught the wind, making the boat lurch forward.

Miguel fell to the deck.

Tulio quickly climbed down. The boat was sailing toward the arch, picking up speed. The cistern was on its way down, winning the battle against the rope-pullers.

Tulio crouched next to his old friend. Miguel was uninjured—that was a relief. Part of Tulio wanted to whoop with joy, to leap up with Miguel in a perfectly timed high-five like the old days. Then, shoulder to shoulder, they would turn to the bow and face whatever came next.

But these were not the old days. His friend wanted to stay in El Dorado, and no matter how much it hurt, Tulio had to let him. When the cistern fell, Miguel would be pushed through the gate with Tulio and Chel. El Dorado would lose not one, but two gods.

"Get off the boat, Miguel," Tulio said, "or you'll never see the city again!"

But Miguel didn't move an inch. "I know," he replied calmly, a smile growing slowly across his face. "You don't think I'm going to let *you* have all the fun, do you? Come on, we've got a wave to catch!"

Tulio grinned. Miguel was with him again. Like the old days.

But there was no time for emotion. As the boat sailed under the great arch, the cistern toppled behind them with a thundering crash.

It cracked open, and water gushed outward in a violent wake that jolted the boat forward. Waves slammed the boat fore and aft in the narrow tunnel.

Chel steered the rudder, keeping them on course in the raging current. They were swiftly approaching the other end of the tunnel. Soon they could see the two massive pillars that supported the narrow exit near the waterfall.

"We're going to have to hit it broadside!" Tulio shouted.

"That's your plan?" Miguel yelled. "But—the gold?"

"I know, I know—just turn the boat!"

Chel yanked on the rudder. Tulio and Miguel used oars to maneuver the boat. It quickly turned sideways. It was longer by far than the width of the exit—

"*On impact, everybody jump!*" Tulio commanded.

The boat hit sharply and jammed in the archway. Tulio, Miguel, Chel, Altivo, and Bibo flew forward through the pillars. Behind them, the gold tumbled out into the water.

The pillars let out an unearthly groan as the stones shifted against each other.

Then, in an avalanche, they collapsed. The earth rumbled. Without the support of the pillars, the tunnel could not withstand its own weight. Boulders fell to the water, sending up tremendous waves. The boat crumpled under the weight like a sack of twigs, burying the gold beneath.

A wave tossed all five passengers into the river.

In moments, the tunnel was sealed. In its place was a

deadfall of rock and trees. The waterfall was nothing more than a trickle.

"We made it!" Tulio exclaimed, rising to his feet. "It worked! It worked!"

Out of the corner of her eye, Chel spotted movement in the trees. She grabbed Tulio by the ear and pulled him down. "Quiet. Get down. There they are."

She and Bibo scampered behind a pile of fallen rocks.

"No…" a deep voice grumbled from the direction of the river—a voice familiar to the hidden group.

Tzekel-Kan's.

"You lying heathen!" answered another voice. "There is nothing here at all!"

Tulio knew who the other speaker was. So did Miguel and Altivo.

Hernan Cortes had arrived.

"No!" Tzekel-Kan pleaded. "Wait! *Wait!*"

Cortes kicked Tzekel-Kan into the water. "Men, seize him! There is no El Dorado here!"

Tzekel-Kan shrieked in protest as two soldiers grabbed his arms. Desperately he glanced over his shoulders—and caught sight of Chel and Bibo.

They waved good-bye.

"No! No, wait!" Tzekel-Kan yelled. "WAAAAAAIIT!"

Tulio and Miguel joined Chel behind the rocks. Raising their arms triumphantly, they screamed with joy, as Bibo and Altivo looked on approvingly.

"Now *that* was an adventure!" Miguel said.

"Yes…yes it was," Tulio replied. He replayed the final

moments in his mind, suddenly remembering what had been lost. Breaking into sobs, he wailed, "And it was *SO MUCH GOLD*!"

Miguel and Chel put their arms around him. They'd all lost their gold too. They knew how he felt.

Altivo glanced down sheepishly at his gleaming gold horseshoes. Quickly, quietly, he tucked his feet behind a rock.

"I'm...fine," Tulio said, sniffling.

"Good." Chel kissed his cheek. "Let's go."

She headed for Altivo, leaving Miguel and Tulio together, alone.

Miguel offered his hand. Tulio just stared at it skeptically.

"Partner?" Miguel said tentatively.

Tulio stood up and clasped Miguel's hand. "Partner."

Arms around each other's shoulders, they ambled toward Chel.

"Hey, guys, come on!" Chel shouted. "You don't want to stay here forever, do you?"

"But we don't have a map," Miguel said.

"We don't have a plan," Tulio added.

"That's what makes it interesting!" Chel insisted.

Tulio liked the sound of that. "You know, she's right."

"What are we waiting for?" Miguel cried out.

The two men jumped onto Altivo.

"Let's follow that trail!" Chel said.

She dug her heels into Altivo. He took off with a powerful lurch—and Tulio and Miguel fell off.

"Come on, boys!" Chel called out. "Yee-hah!"

"Hey! Hey, Altivo!" Tulio scrambled down the path after the horse, with Miguel close behind. *"Excuse me!"*

Laughing, Chel disappeared into the underbrush with Altivo. The adventurers would catch up to her soon enough. And who knew what adventure they might find next.